**Jackie Ashenden** writes dark, emotional stories, with alpha heroes who've just got the world to their liking only to have it blown wide apart by their kick-ass heroines. She lives in Auckland, New Zealand, with her husband, the inimitable Dr Jax, two kids and two rats. When she's not torturing alpha males and their gutsy heroines she can be found drinking chocolate martinis, reading anything she can lay her hands on, wasting time on social media or being forced to go mountain biking with her husband. To keep up to date with Jackie's new releases and other news sign up to her newsletter at jackieashenden.com.

## Also by Jackie Ashenden

*The Spaniard's Wedding Revenge*
*The Italian's Final Redemption*
*The World's Most Notorious Greek*
*The Innocent Carrying His Legacy*
*The Wedding Night They Never Had*

## The Royal House of Axios

*Promoted to His Princess*
*The Most Powerful of Kings*

Discover more at millsandboon.co.uk.

# PREGNANT BY THE WRONG PRINCE

JACKIE ASHENDEN

MILLS & BOON

First published in Great Britain 2021
by Mills & Boon, an imprint of HarperCollins*Publishers* Ltd,
1 London Bridge Street, London, SE1 9GF

www.harpercollins.co.uk

HarperCollins*Publishers*
1st Floor, Watermarque Building,
Ringsend Road, Dublin 4, Ireland

Large Print edition 2022

Pregnant by the Wrong Prince © 2021 Jackie Ashenden

ISBN: 978-0-263-29519-1

04/22

FALKIRK COUNCIL LIBRARIES

This one's for Kevan and Dina.

# CHAPTER ONE

'*STOP.*'

The voice came from behind, an avalanche of dark sound, crashing through the cathedral and silencing the bishop utterly.

Amalia De Vita, in the middle of the aisle, on her way to the altar, froze, her heart thudding in her ears.

*He knows.*

The thought was fleeting, icy, causing her hand that was resting on her father's arm to twitch, nearly going to her stomach in an instinctive protective movement. Luckily, she caught herself at the last moment.

It was impossible. He couldn't know. No one did. Not even Matias, her fiancé. She'd kept that precious secret all to herself and she was sure she hadn't let it slip.

At the altar Matias stood, tall and dark and dapper in his expertly tailored morning suit.

He was frowning in her direction, presumably at the owner of that dark, terrible voice.

But Lia didn't turn. She knew who owned that voice already.

Fear crouched like a prey animal deep inside her.

*You should have told him.*

The silence in the cathedral was complete, every one of the hundreds of people in attendance staring at the ornate oak doors.

'This wedding is cancelled,' the voice said, the weight of authority in his tone crushing everyone flat. 'The woman, if you please, De Vita.'

Beside her, Lia's father, the previous King's most trusted advisor, swung around, his whole body stiff with surprise. 'Your Excellency?'

'Rafael?' Matias said at the same time, taking a step forward from the altar. 'What is the meaning of this?'

There was no reply.

Footsteps came from behind her and someone took her arm in a gentle, but very firm grip. A royal guard.

*No.*

Lia trembled as denial coursed through her and she'd ripped her arm from the guard's hold before she could think better of it, her heart nearly beating its way out of her chest.

Her father was looking at her now and she could feel his shock. And no wonder. She was Amalia De Vita, the chosen bride of Matias Alighieri, heir to the throne of Santa Castelia. Why would the royal guard be coming for her?

'Lia?' There was confusion in her father's blue eyes as he looked at the guard and then at her.

Of course he'd be confused. But she hadn't been able to bring herself to tell him the truth. His disappointment in her would have been more than she could bear.

*He'll find out anyway now.*

Yes, he would.

Lia stayed silent, staring out through the fine gauze of her veil, tension crawling through her.

Perhaps if she didn't move this all might go away. *He* might go away.

Matias was drawing closer, anger written

all over his handsome face. His groomsmen were standing at the altar, muttering among themselves while the bishop looked on disapprovingly.

Whispers, amplified by the magnificent acoustics of the cathedral, moved like a wind through the assembled aristocracy of Santa Castelia.

A scandal in the making. They'd think all their Christmases had come at once.

Then the whispers died, another profound silence falling.

A footstep echoed. Definite. Unhurried. As if whoever was coming towards her had all the time in the world. As if he didn't care one bit that the attention of the entire nation was centred on him as he interrupted the wedding of the century.

But then he wouldn't care, would he?

Matias might be the Prince and heir, but it was his older half-brother who ruled.

Rafael Navarro, the Spanish bastard. Prince Regent of Santa Castelia.

*Don't turn around. Don't look at him.*

She couldn't. She didn't dare. Because the

minute she did, the second he saw her face and looked into her eyes, he'd know.

She'd never been able to hide anything from him.

*Your father isn't the only one who's going to be disappointed.*

A tremble shook her and she swallowed, trying not to give into her fear.

She was Santa Castelia's Crown Princess, the title she'd been given when her betrothal to Matias had been formalised.

She was pure and good. Well behaved. Respectable. No hint of scandal touched her. No unseemly emotions were evident.

She was above reproach in every way.

The footsteps behind her halted.

Lia still couldn't bring herself to turn. She concentrated instead on the stained-glass rose window above the altar, all blue and red and green.

'Praying to God, Lia?' That voice was much closer now, sounding like a night full of shadows and dark dangerous things waiting to rip her to shreds. 'I wouldn't. I'm not sure he's listening. Not to you, at least.'

She said nothing, unable to hear anything over the frantic beat of her heart.

'Your Excellency,' Gian repeated.

'Silence,' Rafael said casually, his tone bordering on insulting.

Her father knew better than to argue and shut his mouth.

Lia's heart ached and ached. But she still didn't turn. She didn't have the courage. Not here, not now. Not with her father present.

'I see,' Rafael continued. 'So it's to be like this, is it?'

Slowly, footsteps circled her and Lia was filled with the insane urge to turn away and keep turning like a ballerina in a music box, so she'd never have to see him. Never have to look at his face. Never have that rapier-sharp gaze meet hers, cutting everything away, uncovering all her secrets, all her shame.

Not that he didn't know that shame already. There was no other reason for him to stop a wedding that had been years in the planning.

Rafael Navarro might hate scenes and scandals, but it seemed that even he had a line. And she'd just pushed him over it.

*What did you expect? That you could hide this from him?*

Yes, that's exactly what she'd expected. How foolish of her.

She could sense him now, approaching from her right side, and soon he'd be in front of her. Soon he'd see her. Soon he'd know everything.

There was no hiding from Rafael, she knew that now.

Her only hope was to pray that she was wrong, that he had some other reason for stopping the marriage of the heir to the throne in full view of an entire nation. A reason that didn't have anything to do with her.

*Keep telling yourself that...*

She braced herself, clutching her bouquet in a death grip, and lifted her chin. At least the veil offered her some protection; she'd be grateful for small mercies.

Rafael stopped in front of her, blocking her view of the altar and Matias, so that all she could see was the wide expanse of his chest.

She swallowed, trying not to shake.

She'd forgotten how tall he was. How massive. How…immovable. He was a man built out of the most adamant of materials, granite and steel and iron. A man who could withstand any shock, any disaster. She'd been a teenager when he'd come to take his place as Regent and everyone had been terrified of him.

His background had been as a CEO of a multi-billion-dollar company, but he'd never looked like a CEO. He'd looked like a general, a warlord. A leader of armies. Dark, frightening, and dangerous, he made the palace guards seem like children merely playing at being soldiers.

*He's not like that, though. Not really.*

But that was her stupid heart doing the talking. The heart that had been somehow fascinated by the much older brother of the man she was supposed to marry. The heart that had nothing to do with the lovely, well-behaved daughter of Gian and Violetta De Vita, who'd been brought up and moulded to be the perfect queen. A heart that was dangerous, rebellious, passionate…

*And stupid.*

Lia stared at that chest, the dove-grey material of his morning suit stretched as it was over rock-hard muscle and bone.

Something quivered inside her.

She didn't want to look up, but if she didn't that would signal she had something to hide and he'd know. Then again, he already knew that passionate, dangerous side of her, so what did she have to lose?

*You're a coward.*

Yes, she'd been that, too. But maybe not today.

Lia took a breath and then lifted her gaze to his from behind her veil.

The air in her lungs froze solid.

He wasn't handsome, but then handsomeness was an irrelevant term when it came to the Regent of Santa Castelia. His black hair was cut short and close to his skull, his face all rough planes and hard angles that somehow came together in a way that was both utterly compelling, yet terrifying at the same time.

A man with charisma and an authority that

made people want to obey simply through the sheer force of his presence alone.

But it wasn't his face that struck the fear of God into her heart.

It was his eyes.

Deep-set below winged black eyebrows, they were a light, crystalline grey. Like silver. Like the edge of a sword or a scalpel, sharp enough to cut. To draw blood.

Impossibly beautiful eyes.

Eyes that saw the truth.

Lia couldn't breathe.

Rafael lifted his hands and grasped the fine silk of her veil, drawing it up and over her face, taking away that last barrier. So there was nothing between herself and the sharp edge of his gaze.

Nowhere to run.

Nowhere to hide.

The expression on his face was impossible to read. But his eyes…they blazed like molten mercury.

'Did you think you could get away with it?' His voice was quiet and somehow even more terrible than when it had been louder. 'Did you think I wouldn't notice?'

Lia couldn't have spoken if her life had depended on it. There was a roaring in her ears. All the air in the cathedral had vanished, as though she was standing in an airlock and someone had opened it straight into a hard vacuum.

There was nothing but darkness and ice, and that relentless silver gaze cutting into her.

'Rafael,' Matias said from behind Rafael's massive shoulders, clearly oblivious to his brother's frozen rage. 'What is happening? You were supposed to be here two hours ago.'

But Rafael didn't turn. He didn't acknowledge his brother in any way. He only looked at Lia as if he'd like to crush her where she stood.

'You will come with me,' he said in that same casually arrogant tone. 'And you will come without a fight.'

She swallowed, desperately trying to find her voice. 'But I—'

He leaned in slightly, looming over her, his mouth near her ear, that terrible voice dropping even lower, so she felt it in her chest. 'Unless, of course, you wish all of Santa Castelia to know that the baby you're carrying isn't my brother's.'

Lia nearly let go of her bouquet of white roses, a rush of the most intense heat flashing through her, closely followed by a wash of ice.

*Did you really think you could keep it a secret for long?*

No, not for long. Just until the wedding. Just until she could tell Matias, who would be surely understanding. Theirs wasn't a love match after all, but something arranged between her father and King Carlos, a long time ago when they were children.

But it was too late for that now.

She felt dizzy, sick. Her brain struggled through a morass of shock, trying to figure out how she'd let it slip, or whether the doctor she'd crossed the border into Italy to see had somehow told someone…

More whispers were rustling through the cathedral, people getting restless, wanting to know what was going on. Why had the Regent so abruptly called a halt to the wedding? And why was he talking to the bride? What terrible, delicious thing could it be?

*You have no choice. You have to go with him. No one else can know your shame.*

She could feel her father next to her, feel his shock and his confusion. He'd want to know what was happening, too, and what would he think when he found out? What about her mother? What would they say when they discovered how badly she'd let them down?

Her cheeks were burning and she wanted to cry, but somehow she found the strength to look into those terrible silver eyes.

She'd deny it. She'd tell him that he was wrong. She'd demand a test, get him to prove it—

'No.' The word was an anvil, crushing all her fight before she'd even had the chance to speak. 'There will be no denial. Just as there will be no escape. There is nowhere you can run to and there is nowhere for you to hide. Not from me, *princesa*.' He smiled and it turned her heart into a block of ice. 'I am inevitable.'

\* \* \*

Rafael Navarro had never considered himself a good man. Good wasn't really in his nature. What was in his nature was a certain facility—some would say genius—with money, impeccable attention to detail, and the iron will required to run a tiny, mountainous nation sandwiched between Spain and Italy with relentless efficiency.

Oh, and he preferred to get his way in all things.

He was also a man who hated shocks, despised surprises and loathed plans that did not proceed in the direction he wished them to go, and right now he was furious, even though fury was not something he customarily allowed himself. Then again fury was the only logical response to the past two hours.

Two hours that had contained nothing but shocks, surprises and seemingly his entire life upended and very much not according to his plan, and all because of the woman standing in front of him.

A small, delicate woman wearing an eye-wateringly expensive confection of a bridal gown that he knew the price of down to the last euro, made of the finest white silk, hand-embroidered with silver thread and tiny crystals. He knew the price of her embroidered gossamer silk veil and the circlet of diamonds on her glossy black hair, the Alighieri ruby on her hand and the small hand-made silver slippers on her feet.

He knew the price of this entire wedding fiasco and the price of its cancellation, too.

Her fault.

It was she who'd upended his perfectly ordered life, she who'd ruined it, and he should have known from the minute he'd laid eyes on her that she would end up costing him.

And now he would make her pay for it.

*It's not* entirely *her fault.*

An inconvenient thought that he ignored, watching instead with some satisfaction the fear that glowed in her deep blue eyes.

She should be afraid. There would be a reckoning and it would be now.

Her face was white, the make-up that was supposed to highlight the serene perfection of her features unable to hide her sickly pallor.

Even so, she was beautiful. Delicate, black arched brows and lush, silky black lashes. A sinful mouth tinted the prettiest shade of pink. A pointed chin that he knew from experience could be forceful and stubborn.

She was not the good, quiet, well-behaved girl she was reputed to be and he'd known that the night he'd caught her in her father's office, drinking his whisky and smoking one of his cigars.

He should have informed Gian then, but he hadn't.

Matias had been due to take the throne in six months and Amalia De Vita had spent her entire life in training to be his wife. There hadn't been another woman more suitable to be Santa Castelia's queen. The De Vita family was an ancient lineage, bringing nobility and pedigree to a throne sorely damaged by the antics of Rafael's father, King Carlos, and Rafael had agreed early on that no other woman would do.

This marriage was supposed to be his last gift to the country that had never warmed to him even as they'd begged him to rule after his father had died.

A lesser man would have used the opportunity to teach them a lesson in being grateful, but Rafael had never been a lesser man. He was above such petty concerns as revenge.

However…

Cold fury shifted inside him as he looked down into Amalia's deep blue eyes, even as it warred with a grudging respect.

She was afraid, yet that forceful little chin was lifted and set. 'There is no need for all the theatrics, Your Excellency,' she said in that low, well-modulated voice that he knew wasn't hers. 'If you want me to come with you, then I will. I just don't want to be dragged out of my own wedding by a palace guard.'

Gian De Vita's face was a mask of very real confusion. It was clear Lia hadn't told him anything, which was probably a small mercy. He'd never approved of Rafael, even if he'd been the one to beg Rafael to be Regent until Matias came of age, and this would not endear him to Gian any further.

Too bad.

He had nothing to lose. The wedding was in ruins now. He'd worked hard for the past six years of his regency to keep the peace in Santa Castelia, to make up for the decades of scandal and profligacy that had characterised his father's reign.

He'd wanted to set an example of restraint and decorum, and he had.

Only for it to end like this.

No, he had nothing to lose. The crown had never been his and it never would. And now he'd caused the kind of scandal he would have abhorred even a week ago.

But everything was different now.

The pure, good girl wasn't quite so pure after all and she'd been hiding a secret. A secret from him.

Well, she couldn't hide it any more.

He'd broken his own vow and he'd done so spectacularly by coming here. Might as well end it in the same way, in the time-honoured fashion.

'In that case,' Rafael said, 'if you don't wish to be dragged from the cathedral by a guard, you shall be dragged from the cathedral by me.' And before anyone could move or say a word, he picked her up, flung her over his shoulder and strode down the aisle to the doors, her veil drifting out behind them, leaving the entire cathedral in an uproar.

At the kerb, the limo that had brought him here was still waiting as instructed, the driver standing with the door open.

Anton didn't appear in the least bit fazed to see the Regent striding down the cathedral steps with the bride over one shoulder. He simply waited until Rafael had deposited Lia inside and got in himself, then shut the door.

Rafael made a mental note to give his driver a substantial raise as the limo took off.

Lia sat on the seat opposite him in a drift of sparkling white tulle, her veil tangled, her diamond circlet hanging lopsidedly over one ear.

She wasn't pale any more and neither was she afraid.

Her cheeks were red with outrage and fury burned in her blue eyes.

*Dios,* she was beautiful when she lost the veneer of manners that her parents had drummed into her.

She said nothing. She only lifted her bouquet and threw it at him.

He caught it before it hit him in the face, the roses showering white petals all over his morning suit. If anyone looked through the windows of the limo now and didn't know who they were, they would have seen a beautiful bride and her new husband, perhaps having a fun game.

They were not having a fun game.

Rafael gently laid the bouquet down on the seat beside him. 'What were you saying about theatrics?'

'How dare you?' she burst out, that clear, well-modulated voice not so clear or so well-modulated any longer, but vibrating with a low, husky rage. 'In front of the entire country! In front of Matias and my father! How dare you even touch me!'

Rafael didn't reply. Sometimes saying nothing said more than a hot tirade, so he calmly picked rose petals from his suit and arranged them in a pattern beside the bouquet, letting her shout at him until she finally ran out of steam.

Then he lifted his head and met her furious blue gaze. 'Have you finished?'

'No!'

He ignored her. 'Good, now it's time we had a little talk.'

'A little talk? A little talk about what?'

'About your pregnancy,' he said. 'About the fact that you've been trying to hide it for months. Specifically about the fact that you've been trying to hide it from *me*.'

'You?' she demanded, her chin lifting. 'And why on earth would I try to hide it specifically from you?'

Rafael stared at her. She was trying to brazen it out, that much was clear.

'Why?' he echoed coldly. 'Because that baby is mine, Lia. Why else?'

# CHAPTER TWO

LIA SAT VERY still, every part of her trembling inside with rage and fear. Rage that he'd picked her up in the middle of the cathedral in front of Matias, her father, the bishop, the entirety of Santa Castelia's aristocracy, not to mention the rest of the country viewing the wedding via a live broadcast, and thrown her over his shoulder as if she weighed nothing. Then had carried her off like a...marauder.

Fear about what he would do now he knew what she'd been hiding from him for three months. What she'd felt she had no choice but to hide from him, because what else was she to do?

She'd made a terrible, *terrible* mistake and there had been consequences, and all of it was her fault. And even though her instinct was to keep denying it, tell him she had no idea her baby was his, she knew she couldn't.

He knew the truth about her, he always had.

It took a tremendous amount of effort to shove down both her rage and her fear, but she'd had years of practice at keeping her wilder emotions in check and so she managed. Throwing her bouquet at him had been a stupid loss of control and she couldn't afford another.

It didn't help that she could still feel the imprint of his hard, muscular shoulder against her stomach, the heat of his body penetrating every layer of her bridal gown. Making her remember that night three months ago when there had been nothing between them but bare skin and raw, aching passion…

No, she couldn't think of that. Not now. Now with his icy silver gaze on her, fury burning coldly in the depths.

'What?' He went on in that insultingly casual way she so hated. 'Not going to deny it again? Perhaps you're going to tell me that you didn't know it was me in bed with you that night? Perhaps you thought it was a stranger, since that's clearly preferable to sleeping with me. Come, *princesa*, tell me. I'm all ears.'

Her voice wouldn't work. She wanted to wind down the window, get some of the snowy winter air into the car just so she could breathe. Because she felt as though she was choking while he just sat there and stared at her the way he'd always stared at her. As if he could see inside her, right down to her soul.

'I have a paternity test,' he continued when she didn't speak. 'If you'd like to see it.'

A paternity test. He'd done a paternity test.

'Why?' The word was hoarse, part of her irrationally furious at him for needing proof. Even though she hadn't even told him about the pregnancy. Even though she'd acted as though their night together had never happened. She'd had to. They'd both had to.

He didn't move, that terrible silver gaze glittering. 'Because I didn't know whether I was the only lucky recipient of your midnight visits. I had to be sure the child was mine.'

Lia had been brought up to be poised and graceful in all things. To be serene and ladylike. Well behaved and unfailingly polite.

Yet in that instant the control that had been drummed into her every day of her life broke apart and shattered like delicate crystal.

All the fear and distress that had been her constant companion over the last three months, all her agony and rage suddenly rose up in a choking wave. She wanted to cry, but crying would solve nothing. And it wasn't really him she was angry at, but herself.

She should have told him the instant her pregnancy test had come back positive. She should have found the courage to face him, to take responsibility for the mistake she'd made. And to face the consequences.

Or better yet, she should never have allowed her anger to get the better of her and gone to what she thought was Matias's room in the first place.

But she hadn't…

*Lia couldn't sleep. She'd been staring out of the window of her bedroom for hours, her heart nothing but a ball of barbed wire in her chest. It had been a couple of weeks since Rafael had stopped coming to those meetings in her father's study and she missed him. She missed him as if she was missing part of herself.*

*He was avoiding her and she didn't understand why. All she knew was that it hurt.*

*Behind her on the bed in a pool of deep blue silk was the gown she was supposed to wear tomorrow night to the ball where her engagement to Matias would be formally announced.*

*She couldn't even look at it. Every time she did, all she could see was her future laid out before her. Her future as the wife of a man who didn't love her and whom she didn't love. Her future as the virtuous Queen of Santa Castelia.*

*A future that felt like the bars of a cage closing slowly around her.*

*It was him. He was the problem. He was the reason she couldn't bear that future now and she didn't know what to do about it. Not that there was anything to be done.*

*She was the Crown Princess. She'd been promised to Matias since she was a child and her role was set in stone. Her father had al-*

*ways been very clear that after the excesses of King Carlos's rule Santa Castelia needed a firm and steady hand. Matias would be that hand and she his steadying influence.*

*Together they would steer Santa Castelia out of the storms of scandal and greed and corruption, and into calmer waters.*

*She was her parents' late-in-life child. Their IVF miracle. Much loved and much wanted, and she shouldn't complain, especially when some children never got to be loved at all.*

*But sometimes the weight of all that expectation was a burden. Miracles were supposed to do wondrous things and her parents had certainly expected wonders from her. She would be a queen because of the work her father had put into negotiating a betrothal with Matias, not to mention all the effort her mother had put into schooling her behaviour and moulding her into the perfect choice of a royal bride.*

*They expected all their hard work to pay off and she couldn't let them down.*

*Yet tonight was a night when she didn't feel like a miracle. Where she felt weighed down by all the expectations placed on her, crushed beneath them, and the ache in her heart, the longing that wouldn't leave her no matter how hard she tried to ignore it. The desperate and confusing desire for a man she could never, ever have, not when only one man was permitted to her.*

*She turned and stared at the gown, the anger she always tried so hard to keep control of licking up inside her.*

*Anger at her parents and what they expected of her.*

*Anger at herself for wanting what she couldn't have.*

*Anger at him because every night for the past two weeks she'd waited in her father's study the way she always did, expecting him to arrive. And he never did. And she didn't know why.*

*She should know better than to give in to her anger, but tonight it felt like too much. She wanted to do something, wanted to hurt him the way he was hurting her. Get rid of this terrible ache inside her somehow.*

*A sheltered girl, he'd called her at their*

*last meeting, his silver eyes burning with an emotion she didn't understand. She'd been furious with him, wanting to deny it, but naturally she couldn't.*

*She was sheltered.*

*Was that why he hadn't come back? Because she was sheltered? Because she was too innocent? Too well bred? And if so, why did that matter to him?*

*Her anger tightened into a hard knot.*

*Well, perhaps she'd show him just how sheltered she really was.*

*The palace was quiet as she stepped out into the corridors, most people asleep. It was so very late and the corridors were dim. She hadn't been to the private wing where the royal family had their rooms very often, but she thought she knew the way.*

*The guards knew her and let her through, and so she'd crept down yet more dark hallways until she found Matias's door.*

*There was no physical attraction between them. They were more friends than anything else, but tonight she would change that.*

*It was Matias she needed to be thinking*

*about. Matias she should want. Matias, not Rafael. And there was only one way she could think of to get rid of these inappropriate desires.*

*She would forget Rafael in the arms of her husband-to-be.*

*The room beyond was in darkness, but she didn't turn on the light. She couldn't risk him sending her away. Instead, she found the bed, let her robe fall and slipped naked between the sheets.*

*The male figure in the bed stiffened in shock as she touched him, waking him up. She heard him take a breath to speak, but in the dark she found his mouth and laid a finger over it. It was soft beneath her touch.*

*'Don't talk,' she whispered, staring at the shape of the man next to her. 'It's only me. Please, I know it's wrong to be here, but... I need you.'*

*Matias didn't say anything, staying still for a long moment. Then he grabbed her and kissed her like a man possessed.*

*And as soon as his mouth covered hers, her*

*brain finally caught up with what her body
had already recognised.*

*The man she was kissing wasn't Matias.*

*It was Rafael.*

Rafael, who generated so many confusing
and tortured emotions inside her.

Rafael, who she desired so much it made
her ache.

Rafael, who now seemed to assume that his
wasn't the only bedroom she'd visited.

Normally when her feelings got the better
of her, she went out for a walk in the palace
gardens, but she couldn't do that now. She
was trapped in a car with him. Trapped in the
wild flood of her own emotions. All the unre-
quited passion and fear. All the choking rage
that she had nowhere to direct but at him.

Lia lunged across the space between them
before she could stop herself, no thought in
her head but lash out at the most convenient
target.

He seemed to be expecting it, however.
Before she could land any kind of blow, he
grabbed her wrists with insulting ease and

hauled her on to his lap, her skirts bunched between them and flowing over the black leather seats of the limo.

Lia found herself staring into his eyes, the muscular heat of his body surrounding her, and abruptly she was trembling yet again, her body recognising his, her anger alchemising into something much hotter.

'I had to know, *princesa*,' Rafael said now in his hard, dark voice, his gaze blazing into hers, reading her mind as easily as if she was a book spread open before him. 'You cannot blame me for that. Especially when you didn't tell me.'

Lia shivered 'I… I thought it was Matias. I went to his room. I thought it was him in the bed…'

Rafael's gaze went molten as it raked over her. Then his expression twisted in what looked like a snarl and she found herself pushed hard away, deposited back firmly in the seat opposite him.

He pressed a button in the seat arm next to him and said something harsh and guttural in Spanish.

Lia's hands were cold and so were her toes. Shock, probably.

She didn't know what to do with herself. This morning when she'd woken up, she was the bride-to-be for Santa Castelia's Crown Prince and now...

*You failed. You failed your fiancé. Your country. Your parents. And you failed* him, *too.*

Her throat closed and she turned her head away from the fierce gaze of the man opposite, staring blindly out the window. The streets and buildings of Santa Castelia's capital were lost under a cloud of white. It was snowing and snowing hard, as if the snow was a living embodiment of Rafael's cold fury.

'I went to Matias's room, because I was trying to forget about you,' she said thickly, because she owed him an explanation and he had to know that it hadn't been—it had *never* been—Matias that she'd really wanted. 'I thought that being with him would...help me.' No point telling him that she'd been angry with him, too, not when that would possibly only inflame things.

'I see.' Rafael's voice was wiped clean of expression. 'And when did you realise you weren't, in fact, in Matias's room? Before or after your first orgasm?'

Anger licked up once again through the shame crowding in her throat, and she turned her head. 'Do you really think I wouldn't know who was touching me?'

He didn't look away. 'It was dark. And you clearly had no idea where Matias's rooms were. You could have walked into anyone's.'

'And I would have left the second I realised I was with just anyone,' she shot back. 'But I wasn't. I was with you.'

'Would you have stayed if it hadn't been? If it had been Matias in the bed instead of me?'

She shouldn't challenge him, not now, not here. Yet she couldn't help herself. Her emotions were all over the place, as they had been ever since she'd met him, and even more now she was pregnant. 'Do you really want to know the answer to that?'

Rafael's features were as uncompromising

as his stare. 'I wouldn't have asked otherwise.'

She wanted to say 'yes, I would have stayed', because part of her wanted to hurt him. To get back at him for the situation she'd found herself in, for the months of mental anguish she'd gone through after finding out she was pregnant, for how he'd stopped coming to see her without explanation, for all the confusing emotions she felt whenever she was around him. Emotions she shouldn't be having about a man who'd never been hers and wasn't supposed to be.

But she *had* to control herself. Everything was too close to the surface already and Rafael had always been the spark to her dry tinder. He made her catch alight, made her burn. He got under her skin and she couldn't allow it.

The future she'd always thought she'd have might have been torn from her after today, but that was no excuse to let herself slip back into old patterns.

If the last three months had taught her anything, it was that she could *not* give in to her own wants and desires. That was selfish.

*But why not? What does it matter? Who do you have to perform for now?*

The thought whispered in the back of her mind, but she ignored it. Everything felt too precarious right now and at least the role of the Crown Princess was one she was familiar with. That, she could do.

'I don't know,' she said more carefully. 'It's a moot point now, anyway.'

Rafael's harsh features betrayed nothing, but she could feel the fury radiating from him all the same. A cold fury, though. So cold she was almost surprised it wasn't actually snowing inside the car.

'My turn then.' Ice threaded through his tone, his anger frozen over. 'I always knew it was you. Right from the moment you woke me.'

Lia swallowed, her throat closing. She'd kept herself rigidly locked down for the past three months, refusing to think about him or that night. Trying not to give in to her own fear and shame. But sometimes she'd find her thoughts straying to him, wondering what that night had meant to him. Whether he'd been as changed by it as she had or whether he viewed it as just another night.

Whether she'd been just another woman.

Her heart clenched tight. 'Rafael…'

'I should have stopped. I should have resisted. But you said "I need you". And then you kissed me as though you were drowning and I had all your air.'

She shut her eyes, the memory of that kiss burning in her mind like a brand. The moment his lips had touched hers, she'd gone up in flames.

'I didn't—'

'I thought you'd come to find *me*, Lia. I thought it was me you wanted.'

There was so much fury in his voice. It hurt. 'I told you, I was trying to forget you—'

'The next day,' he went on as if she hadn't spoken, 'you became officially engaged to my brother. And at that ball, you looked at me as if I was some dirt you found underneath your pretty little shoe.'

Oh, god. Was that what he'd thought?

* * *

*Rafael was a tall, imposing figure in his black evening clothes, his only adornment the heavy gold ring of state—he'd drawn every eye in the ballroom. He was the still point about which the world turned and she hated it that, despite the intensity of the night before, her world still revolved around him.*

*She'd thought the night before, experiencing all that physical passion, would have changed things, would have made her want him less, but it hadn't. If anything, it had made her want him more.*

*Now she knew what she'd been missing, now she knew what they could have had together. So much pleasure that could have been hers if he hadn't been who he was and if she hadn't been engaged to his brother.*

*Being in his presence was difficult, yet she didn't have a choice. She couldn't not attend the ball thrown in her and Matias's honour, just as Rafael had to be there to give his blessing.*

*Normally his acknowledgement of her was cool and casual, but not tonight. Tonight, he stared at her, with so much intensity it nearly flattened her.*

*She'd been so terrified of giving herself away it was all she could do to curtsy and murmur, 'Your Excellency...' before excusing herself and fleeing.*

Lia's heart twisted. 'I didn't—'

'I knew then it was for the best,' he interrupted once more, still coldly furious. 'To keep the night we'd shared as just a night. And it would never be spoken of again. So, I put it from my mind. But a few weeks later I remembered that I hadn't used a condom. You hadn't contacted me, though, so I assumed it wasn't a problem.' He said it casually, as if none of this meant anything at all to him. 'Then I had reports you weren't well. That you were attending social engagements, but were pale and obviously hadn't been sleeping.'

She hadn't been. The morning sickness had been brutal and it had taken everything she had just to function normally. Her mother had been worried about her getting sick so close to the wedding, but she'd told her it was merely a stomach bug.

'So I made some enquiries.' Rafael's accent, lilting and melodic, had haunted her dreams for the past two years, but it did nothing to soften the hard edge in his voice. 'It seems you'd gone to a different doctor, not the one your family normally uses. That made me suspicious. From there it was relatively easy to discover the reason for it.'

The cold began creeping up her arms and up her legs. 'She wouldn't have told you.'

His expression was as unyielding as granite. 'She would. She did. Everyone has a price. Even doctors.'

'I don't—'

'It was simple to get a strand of your hair for DNA purposes. The paternity test was a match.'

'Rafael.'

'I found out today that I was going to be a father.' The words were heavy as iron, cutting her off cold. 'Only hours before you were going to marry my brother.'

'But I—'

*'Silence.'*

His anger filled the car, as icy as the blizzard outside, making her shiver. If she let out a breath, she was sure she'd be able to see it.

'You have known for months and you *hid* it. You were going to marry my brother and pass *my* child off as his.' His hard mouth, that had felt so warm and soft beneath hers, that had given her so much pleasure, twisted in a sneer. 'Did you want him to be the father? Did you have doubts about me? Is that why didn't tell me you were pregnant?'

'No!' She curled her hands into fists to stop them from shaking. His assumption that she'd doubt him hurt, but she knew she had no one to blame for that but herself. 'I didn't tell you, because I was afraid. Because I was engaged to your brother and Santa Castelia needed the marriage.'

The fury in his eyes didn't change. 'How unfortunate for us both then that I discovered your little secret.' He leaned forward very slightly, his terrible gaze sharp as a scimitar, cutting right through her soul. 'But don't worry. Regardless of my feelings on the subject, it's not going to stay a secret much longer. Not when from now on you and the baby are mine.'

She'd gone white as a sheet and, deep inside him, Rafael felt something shift. But he ignored it. He was too angry with her to feel any kind of sympathy.

Not only had she hidden her pregnancy from him for months, if what she'd said was true then that night it hadn't even been him she'd been looking for.

She'd been looking for his brother.

For three months he'd watched the wedding preparations, fighting not only the jealousy that dogged him, but also the desire that burned in his blood whenever she was near. Consoling himself with the knowledge that, though she was marrying Matias, it had been him she'd come to that night.

It had been him she'd wanted.

But, no, apparently not.

The only thing she'd wanted was to forget him.

His anger was a bonfire, but he knew the

dangers so he froze it solid, turning it to sharp ice. Anger could be a good fuel if used prudently and he was nothing if not prudent. His whole life had been built on it.

And while she might have turned that life upside down, he wasn't going to let her cause any more damage than she already had. Someone had to fix it and he was nothing if not good at fixing things.

He shouldn't have taken such a drastic course of action, but she'd forced him into it. By not telling him about her pregnancy, he'd only had a week or so to investigate and even then he'd only learned about the results of the paternity test a mere hour before the wedding.

That had left him with only one option. He had to stop her from marrying Matias any way he could. Unfortunately, his anger had got the better of him and he'd stopped the wedding in the most disruptive way possible.

Yet what else could he have done? Matias hadn't known about her pregnancy, Rafael was positive. And this was a mess that he'd made himself. He couldn't allow his brother to take responsibility for something that was none of his doing. He couldn't allow any doubt to be cast on the heir to the throne either, not after the scandals of their father's reign.

And apart from all that, Lia's baby was also his and he would not allow another man to claim it, even if that man was his brother.

He'd had no intention of having children, not after his own bleak upbringing, but now that decision had been taken out of his hands, he knew he couldn't let his own child grow up without someone to set them a good example. Not with the genes they'd no doubt inherited.

His own father, King Carlos, had been known for his baser appetites and profligate ways. Rafael, after all, had been a direct product of that appetite, his mother a hotel chambermaid. He'd been brought up in a one-roomed apartment in Barcelona and while he and his mother hadn't lived in dire poverty, they hadn't been far from it. Carlos had paid nothing for his upkeep and Rafael had had no contact with him, except every so often when his father would demand an exclusive audience at one of his residences.

His mother had always been very against him seeing Carlos, but his father had given neither of them a choice. He'd insisted on Rafael's presence, though always in secret since his father wouldn't acknowledge him openly. Awkward meetings where Carlos, depending on his mood, would either heap praise on him for doing well, or barely speak to him at all.

Once, when he'd been twelve, Rafael had asked him what the purpose of these visits was since it was clear that Carlos didn't have any feeling for him.

'Just because I don't acknowledge my mistakes doesn't mean I can't learn from them,' his father had responded coldly.

As if Rafael had needed more confirmation of his own status. He knew he was a mistake. His mother had been quite clear about that.

Regardless, he would never put any child of his through that. Never, *ever.*

Rafael had always prided himself on his control—he'd never be profligate with his affairs as Carlos had been—but controlled was the last thing he'd been when Lia had come to his bed.

He'd made a mistake, it was true. But unlike Carlos he owned that mistake. He took responsibility for it.

So he would claim his child. He would acknowledge them. They would be his and not a mistake to be buried and forgotten about. Or viewed whenever the mood took him. He would be a better father than his own had ever been.

Lia's blue eyes had darkened, her face still as white as her gown.

That thread of sympathy that he'd buried and frozen beneath the layer of his icy rage tugged harder.

*So, she didn't come looking for you that night the way you thought, and she didn't tell you about the baby. Did you even bother to ask her why not? No. You dragged her from her wedding, locked her in this limo and shouted at her.*

Unease twisted deep in his gut.

He'd never been a warm, empathetic man,

but he was never cruel and especially not to a woman, let alone a pregnant one.

Then again, this was what always happened with Lia. She got to him in a way no other woman ever had and so he had to be on his guard.

He'd already made one catastrophic error of judgement and had only compounded it today. There was no need to make any more.

The snow was coming down even harder and the temperature of the car was a little chilly. That gown she wore wouldn't exactly be keeping her warm.

'Are you cold?' he asked, keeping his voice casual, which was his preferred method of modifying himself. 'I'll turn the heat up.' He didn't wait for her to respond, fiddling with the temperature controls until he was satisfied.

She ignored him. 'What do you mean I'm yours? What about Matias?'

The unease inside him twisted harder. So much for the example he'd been trying to set his brother. Moderation, control, cold focus.

The country before all else. He'd modelled exactly none of those things.

Matias wouldn't be so much furious at Lia's loss as he would be at the loss of the future he'd planned. The bride he'd been promised. The upending of everything he'd thought set in stone.

*He never appreciated her for who she was and you know it. He wanted a queen. He didn't want* her.

Possessiveness wound through him, the angry, passionate thoughts that he'd tried so hard to keep buried. Because it was true. Matias liked Lia well enough, but he didn't know the heart of her. She had moderated herself so completely for him that Matias had commented once or twice to Rafael that he found her dull.

But Lia wasn't dull. She was the opposite. Fiery, intense, rebellious. A little impulsive, yet sharp as a knife.

*He doesn't deserve her. But you do.*

Rafael crushed that thought flat. Such entitlement. No one deserved anything. You had to work for it.

'Matias will survive,' he said, focusing on all the things that needed to be done instead of the things that seethed beneath the surface of the ice. 'Leave that to me.'

A new bride would have to be chosen and Lia's parents would have to be compensated. Gian would demand it and that would be expensive. Then again, the treasury was obscenely healthy these days, which was all thanks to him. Santa Castelia could afford it.

It was the finding of a new bride that would be difficult, but that didn't mean one couldn't be found. A bride more suited to Matias's personality than Lia ever was.

The political ramifications, though, would have to be dealt with and quickly. Lia didn't need to be a part of that. He'd take her to his private residence in the mountains and leave her there until he'd handled the fallout.

Then he'd marry her himself. There was no other option.

They'd both made a mistake that night, but the lack of contraception had been his error and his alone. An error that he would fix as soon as possible.

*That's fine. Tell yourself you're marrying her because of all these other things and not because you want her for yourself.*

It was not a particularly pleasant thought, mainly because it brought him face to face with his own baser urges. Urges that for the past fifteen years of his life he'd controlled without effort. Until he'd met her.

Yes, he did want her, he couldn't deny that, and a tiny part of him felt nothing but satisfied at this turn of events. Almost as if fate had delivered her into his hands, which was fanciful of him. Still, fanciful or not, he couldn't refuse that gift. He wouldn't.

'You didn't answer the question. What about me?' She'd modulated her voice into that low, pleasant tone that she used with everyone, clasped her hands in her lap. The Crown Princess back in control.

He wanted to tell her that there was no point in her princess façade now and definitely not with him, but the situation was already flammable and he didn't need to strike another match.

'You? You, I'll take to my residence in the

mountains.' Rafael relaxed back against the seat, extending his arms along the top of it and stretching his legs out so that they nudged her skirts. 'Then I'll go to the palace and inform them of our intended marriage.'

'Our marriage?' Her modulated tone vibrated as she sat bolt upright, every part of her rigid. '*Our* marriage?'

He gave her a long, steady look. 'I'm a bastard, *princesa*. You can't think I'd let our child be born out of wedlock.'

'That's ridiculously medieval, even for you.' A spark glowed in her eyes, the white pallor of her cheeks vanishing under the faint blush of temper. 'It's the twenty-first century, Rafael, in case you'd forgotten. You can't make me marry you if I don't want to.'

Something stirred beneath the ice inside him, something hot and possessive. A recognition of the woman he'd spent so many illicit hours with in Gian's study. The woman she was beneath the gently bred façade of the Crown Princess.

A woman who'd given him the most intense

pleasure he'd ever experienced that night in his bed.

*Dios,* he remembered every single second…

*Rafael strode into the royal chambers and slammed the door shut after him. A bottle of the finest brandy and a glass of cut crystal waited for him on the table beside the overly ornate stone fireplace where a fire roared.*

*The day had been a nightmare. He'd spent it in meetings with his council, which wouldn't have been so bad if the rooms where the meetings had been held hadn't overlooked the gardens of the palace. And if those meetings hadn't coincided with Lia walking in those same gardens.*

*Rafael had had to spend hours trying to pay attention to his meetings, when all his aware-ness centred on the view through the windows of the lovely, lovely woman his brother was going to marry.*

*The woman he'd got to know over the course of months, meeting with her at night in her fa-ther's study. Nothing ever untoward had hap-*

*pened in those meetings. No lines had ever been crossed, but he'd known deep down that it was wrong. That he shouldn't be spending so much time with her alone at night.*

*Yet he'd kept going back, unable to help himself. Drawn by their discussions, by her wit and her intellect. Her fire and her passion, and by the way she looked at him.*

*That last time he'd nearly broken his vow to himself that he wouldn't touch her, and so had made the decision not to go back. And he hadn't.*

*Except he hadn't been able to drag his gaze away from that window, watching the last of the summer sun gloss her black hair as she'd wandered through the gardens...*

Dios, *this obsession with her had to end.*

*She would be marrying Matias and the sooner the better as far as he was concerned.*

*If only the last time they'd met, he hadn't got so close to her. If only he hadn't seen the hunger in her beautiful blue eyes and known that it was for him.*

*That though she might be promised to Ma-*

*tias, the golden boy, it was him she wanted. Him, the bastard Regent his own parents had felt nothing for.*

*And if only he'd looked away and pretended he hadn't seen it.*

*But he hadn't and he didn't, and for long seconds at a time they'd sat there, Gian's desk between them, frozen as their gazes had locked and held.*

*Rafael knocked his brandy back, then paced around. Tried to forget about her by throwing himself into some work. Then, when that failed, he went to bed.*

*Only to be woken in the dark by the familiar scent of a familiar woman and the soft touch of her finger, silencing him. 'Don't talk,' she'd whispered. 'It's only me. Please, I know it's wrong to be here, but... I need you.'*

*And when she reached for him, he didn't think about the last three months of agony. He didn't think about his brother. As soon as her hands touched him he didn't think at all, his much-vaunted self-control lost under a tide of need so acute all he could do was give in...*

* * *

He shifted, his body responding to the memories so strongly it was all he could do not to reach across the space between them and haul her into his lap once again.

'And do you want to marry me?' he only asked in a mild tone.

The blue in her eyes glowed more intensely. 'What do you think? No, I do not.'

# CHAPTER THREE

A STRANGER MIGHT think that Rafael's fury had subsided since his expression now betrayed nothing but mild interest.

Lia knew better. She could see that fury still in his gaze, an icy blizzard that made her breath catch.

The tension in the car had ratcheted up, making every muscle in her body go rigid. She was trying to control her own fury, because seriously, he couldn't think she would agree, could he? That he could kidnap her from her own wedding and then marry her himself, as if all of it was a foregone conclusion?

Except it was clear that he did.

*Why not marry him? Wasn't this what you always secretly hoped for?*

No, of course it wasn't and that was a traitorous thought. She'd never harboured any secret dreams of marriage to anyone, not when she'd always known that the man she would marry was Matias.

Except there was no hope of that now, was there? Matias was out of her reach.

'I see,' Rafael said, in that maddeningly mild tone. 'That is something we can discuss later then. Or would you prefer to argue with me now?'

Actually, she did want to argue with him now. But that would be a mistake with her control still so tenuous. There was too much tension in the air, too much of the past hanging over them, and the topic was too fraught.

Better to leave it until they'd both had a chance to calm down.

She decided not to speak, turning her head away, staring out at the falling snow instead.

The limo was starting to wind up one of the narrow roads that led into the mountains surrounding the capital, stark cliffs looming on either side. The world outside was all black and white and silence.

The temperature in the car had warmed and she felt less cold, though maybe she was imagining that, especially with the after-effects of shock still winding through her.

Certainly, thinking about what would happen between her and Rafael now was selfish, especially given how many other people had been affected by Rafael's actions.

Her parents and their hopes and dreams for her as Queen. Matias and his plans for her as his wife. Santa Castelia itself and the need for a steady, stable king and queen at the helm.

All of that gone.

The thought made her ache.

'My father,' she said at last into the silence. 'We will have to—'

'As I said, I will deal with that.' Rafael's voice was almost negligent. 'Your parents will be compensated.'

'I'm not a horse, Rafael.' She tried not to sound bitter. 'You think money will make up for everything they wanted for me?'

'Will it not?' He raised a black brow. 'Was it you they were thinking of when they promised you to Matias or was it themselves?'

A cold little pulse of yet more shock went

through her. 'What are you talking about? Of course they were thinking of me.'

'Were they? You said you're not a horse and yet you were certainly bred like a brood mare for the role they'd decided on for you.'

Her anger was sitting far too close to the surface and she could feel it start to simmer in response. Because he was wrong. Her parents had spent years trying to conceive and when it had finally happened they'd been so happy. They'd wanted great things for her, because they loved her. She was their miracle.

'Don't be ridiculous.' Anger edged the words no matter how hard she tried not to let it. 'I was not "bred". They wanted a baby and spent years trying for one and when I was finally conceived, they wanted me to have the best life possible.'

'And the best life possible was you being married off to a man you felt nothing for and a role where you'd have to spend the next thirty years pretending to be something you're not.'

Lia felt as though he'd dumped a bucket of ice water over her head.

He just sat there, staring back at her the way

he used to do during those nights they'd spent together, where he'd say something challenging, daring her to refute it. She'd loved it when he did that. It was such a change from the boring etiquette and protocol lessons her mother drilled into her.

Their arguments had never been personal, only intellectual, and they'd made her feel alive somehow. Stimulating in a way the endless lessons in finance and history, deportment, and queenship had never been.

*Because you were bored and he was the only exciting thing in your life.*

He might have been then, but she wasn't bored now and this wasn't exciting. This was distressing.

'You're wrong,' she said flatly. 'Matias and I—'

'Matias and you would have had a perfectly dull marriage,' Rafael interrupted for the millionth time. 'And you would have found being Queen—'

'Perfectly fine,' she snapped, deciding it was time that she interrupted him for a change. 'This conversation is over.'

He lifted one massive shoulder. 'All I'm saying is that your life is what you make it. No one was forcing you to marry my brother. You could have chosen a different path.'

He had an answer for everything, didn't he?

'Easy for you to say. As the Regent of an entire nation.'

His silver eyes gleamed, his hard features not softening one iota. 'I'm a bastard, *princesa*. I grew up on the edge of poverty in Barcelona. I expected nothing and was given nothing. Everything I have, I made. And everything I am, I created for myself. You think your father and Santa Castelia would have come to me if I'd still been that skinny boy grubbing in the gutter? No. They came to me because of what I'd turned myself into.'

*And you turned yourself into their perfect daughter, ready for the role they'd given you. With no thought in your head as to what you wanted for yourself.*

No, that wasn't true. She'd wanted to be Matias's wife and Santa Castelia's Queen. Her parents had so worked hard to give her that future, how could she refuse them? Especially after they'd gone through so much to even have her in the first place.

Plus, she loved her country and she knew she could do good for it. She could help Matias take a different path to that of his notorious father, put the scandals of the past behind them and forge a new future. One where the King and Queen served the country and not the other way around.

*Except in the end you're no better than Carlos was. Falling prey to your own lusts. Putting your own desires ahead of everything else.*

Lia ignored that, very conscious of Rafael's gaze on her and that she had no answer to what he'd just said. Because it was true. Everyone in the world knew Rafael Navarro's background; it had been one of the most talked-about stories of the last five years. How Gian, as the nation's first advisor, had gone begging to the bastard son of King Carlos after he'd died, desperate for someone to take over the disaster that had once been Santa Castelia. Inflation and unemployment had been sky-high, the treasury empty.

Matias had been too young to take over and there was provision for any illegitimate offspring to rule until the legitimate heir came of age.

So they'd come to Rafael, needing his financial genius to save the country and he had. Single-handedly.

But someone needed to ensure its future and Lia had always thought that person would be her, at Matias's side.

Not any more.

Her stomach dipped and hollowed, and she had to look away again, forcing down the riot of violent emotions that churned inside her, struggling to find her usual calm.

She didn't want to talk to Rafael or think about what he'd said, so she didn't, ignoring him as his phone rang a few moments later and he answered it, the dark, rough textures of his voice filling the car.

Twenty minutes later, they turned off the increasingly treacherous mountain road, drove through a pair of massive, wrought-iron gates and went up a winding, equally treacherous driveway. Snow-covered trees loomed on either side, making Lia feel claustrophobic and suffocated. As if she was a prisoner being transported from one prison to another, and this one smaller, darker...

The limo drew up outside what appeared to be a concrete bunker covered in snow. It was only after she'd blinked a few times and told herself not to be so stupid that she realised that it wasn't actually a concrete bunker, but an architectural house made of stone and built against the mountainside in a series of boxes, each on different levels, looking as though they'd been carved out of the mountain itself.

Snow blanketed what in summer would be lovely terraces, making a white carpet on the flat roofs. The house was heavy and monolithic, and, like its owner, looked as if it could withstand any kind of natural disaster thrown at it and then some.

Rafael got out of the car first and held the door open for her. Icy air made her shiver as she collected her skirts and followed him out. Instantly she was freezing, the silver satin slippers she wore ruined as they sank into the snow on the ground. The wind was biting, blowing her skirts and her veil around and making walking difficult. Snow fell everywhere, settling in her eyelashes and falling like white hot sparks on the exposed skin of her shoulders and arms.

Struggling to take a step, she slipped on the icy ground, only to feel a muscular arm slide around her waist, drawing her into the wicked heat of a hard, masculine body.

His scent hit her, warm and spicy and familiar. Unexpected, too, as it always was. In those first few days when he'd come to the palace and she'd been half-terrified, half-fascinated by him, she'd thought that he might smell of cordite or gunpowder, something sharp and dangerous and cold.

But he didn't. He smelled of sandalwood and cloves, making her think of warm nights in a desert, or spices in an exotic souk, fascinating, far-off places that she'd always wanted to visit and yet never had the opportunity.

Oh, God, the last time she'd been this close to him had been that night they'd spent together, his hands on her skin, that same, warm scent surrounding her, setting every nerve-ending she had ablaze with a sudden, insistent heat.

She'd known it was Rafael in that moment and her heart had swelled with happiness and relief. And the terrible knowledge that even if it had been Matias, she would never have been able to go through with her plan to sleep with him.

Because the only man she'd ever wanted was his half-brother.

Lia could feel her body melting into Rafael's heat now, into the strength and power of his hard, muscled torso, the cold that had gripped her fading, vanishing under a wild rush of pent-up physical desire.

Instantly, she tried to pull away, not wanting to give in to it, but his grip on her only tightened. Her skirts trailed in the snow, making it hard for her to take a step even with his help, and so the next minute she found herself swept up into his arms and being carried across the snowy ground to the big black metal front doors of his granite fortress-like house.

She wanted to struggle, to fight the terrible urge to melt against him, because it felt wrong, as though she was giving in somehow, but it was cold and she had to get inside and this was the quickest way.

She held herself rigid, though he didn't seem to notice, much to her irritation.

The door opened for them, a black-uniformed staff member murmuring something in Spanish. Rafael replied in a low tone, but Lia wasn't listening. Because despite how hard and cold the house appeared from the outside, inside it was beautifully warm.

The front entrance was flagged with dark stone, the walls a pale cream, the light warm and welcoming. Used to the clutter of decor in the palace, Lia couldn't help but notice that Rafael's house was comparatively bare and minimalist. There was art on the walls, but it was obvious that each piece had been chosen and placed there with some care. And each piece was beautiful, full of texture and colour: a beautiful landscape in oils, an antique woven tapestry, a rustic pot with a vivid red glaze, an evocative black and white photo.

Rafael turned and carried her down a short hallway and into a big living area where a crackling fire roared in a stark black fireplace. The floor was covered with a nearly black, thick charcoal carpet, the furniture low, comfortable-looking couches upholstered in heavily textured cream linen. The stark black and white decor was softened with jewel-bright rugs, more pieces of carefully chosen art, cushions and discreet lighting.

Rafael carried her over to the couch and deposited her on it—indeed, it was as comfortable as it looked. The staff member—an older woman with white-streaked black hair and dark eyes—had followed them to the door and Rafael spoke again in lilting Spanish.

The staff member nodded and disappeared. Rafael strode to one of the armchairs, picked up a soft throw of deep blue cashmere and carried it over to her, bending to methodically wrap her up in it.

She pulled away, his nearness suddenly too much for her.

His eyes narrowed. 'You're cold.'

'Yes, but believe it or not I can wrap up warmly myself.'

He ignored that, his gaze dropping to her bridal gown, the skirts of which were now wet and clinging unpleasantly to her skin. 'You will need clothing.'

'I'm fine.'

'You are not,' he said in that irritatingly certain way of his. 'You're shivering.'

Annoyingly, he was right.

Lia grimaced and pulled the soft, warm wool tighter around her shoulders. 'I'll be all right in a few minutes.'

His hands fell away and slowly he rose to his full height. He didn't say anything for a long moment, staring at her so intently she almost had to look away. 'How are you feeling? I had reports that you weren't well initially.'

'Morning sickness. It passed.' She felt suddenly very tired, the shock of the past hour starting to take its toll.

'Why didn't you come to me?' His voice

was flat, yet she could hear something vibrating beneath the words, a deeper emotion she couldn't place.

She met his gaze, but his expression gave nothing away. Well, there was no reason not to tell him. She was too tired to argue right now anyway.

'I told you. I was afraid. We shared one night together, Rafael. That's all. And like you, I tried not to think about it, but then I started feeling sick and...' She swallowed, remembering the fear that had gripped her, bone-deep and icy. 'When the test was positive, I didn't know what to do. I...couldn't tell you. You were the Regent, the scandal if anyone found out would have been terrible, and I knew you would have hated that, so I... I thought keeping it secret was better.'

His silver eyes flickered, the lines of his starkly masculine face hardening. 'And yet the secret came out anyway.' There was no compromise in his voice. 'You should have come to me. You could at least have told me that you were pregnant, given me the opportunity to help you.'

Her heart clenched tight in her chest. He was right, she should have. But she'd been too shocked, too upset and, fundamentally, too unsure of his reaction.

'I know I should,' she said. 'But I didn't. We never talked about anything personal those nights in Papa's study and I didn't know how you would feel about it.'

His expression was harsh. 'I would have thought that at least you knew you could trust me.'

Her heart constricted even tighter. 'How could I have known that? I didn't know how you felt about anything.' Unconsciously, her hand had dropped to her stomach in an instinctive, protective movement.

He noticed, the look on his face turning dark. 'You think I'd hurt you? That I'd hurt our son or daughter?'

Pain curled through her. 'No,' she said quickly, because Rafael Navarro was many things, hard and cold and pitiless to the rest of the world, but she knew he would never harm a woman or a child, still less his own. 'No, I know you wouldn't.'

He was silent a minute. 'Did you love him, Lia?' he asked suddenly. 'Did you want to be his wife so badly? Did you want to be his Queen?'

Everything in her ached. Because, no, she hadn't been in love with Matias. And she hadn't been in love with Matias because Rafael had appeared and thrown everything she knew about herself, everything she knew about her own feelings, into disarray.

She didn't want to tell him that, but he might as well know the basic facts.

'No,' she said. 'I didn't love him. But, yes, I wanted to be his wife and I wanted to be Queen. That's what I've spent my whole life training for and you know it. My parents worked so hard to give me that opportunity and I didn't want to let them down.'

He said nothing, simply staring at her, and what he was thinking she had no idea.

*You didn't only let your parents down, but you let* him *down, too. He thought you'd come to him and you hadn't...*

Lia swallowed and then went on, forcing out the painful truth. 'This baby is...my fault,

Rafael. If I hadn't got so angry, I wouldn't have gone to find Matias. I wouldn't have come to you and so all of this wouldn't have happened. It's not your responsibility to fix this.'

Still he said nothing.

'You can't actually want to marry me, Rafael,' she said.

Something in his face shifted. 'You have no idea what I want.' He turned to the door. 'We will discuss this later.'

Then he strode out.

'I'm sorry, Your Excellency, but the road back into the capital is blocked. There is no way to get to the palace, not tonight.'

Rafael glowered at his driver, the anger he'd thought he'd firmly locked down threatening his usual cold focus. Though it wasn't Anton's fault the wretched weather had turned against him.

The Regent grabbing the bride and leaving for his own residence without a word wasn't going to be a great look. It was too much like his father's scandalous behaviour for Rafael's comfort, so he'd wanted at least to show up at the palace in person with an explanation.

However, it looked as though that wasn't going to be an option if the roads were impassable.

'By air?' he asked, even though he knew the answer.

Anton shook his head. 'No, Excellency. Not in this weather.'

Well, that was nothing he didn't already know. And there was one good thing about the weather—if he couldn't get to the palace then at least no one could get to him. Which meant now he had more than enough time to make sure Lia agreed to marry him.

He'd already decided that during the brief moment he'd had with her in the living area, before he'd had to leave to get control of the jealousy and anger he could feel seething under his skin: at her, at his brother, at himself.

He was sure of one thing, though. No matter what she'd said about this being her responsibility, it was his also and he had a duty both to her and his child. And, to him, that meant marriage.

Since he'd taken her from the cathedral in full view of everyone, their relationship would no doubt be in the process of being picked apart. People would put two and two together and come up with four.

Marriage was the only way to save them, to put a gloss of respectability over their illicit encounter and make sure neither she nor their child would be subject to gossip.

But it wasn't only her agreement to a marriage he wanted. He needed to know why she hadn't trusted him enough to come to him. Oh, she'd given him all sorts of reasons— fear, wanting to protect him from scandal, all kinds of things—but in the end it all boiled down to one thing: trust.

*Why are you so surprised? Did you give her any reason to trust you?*

Well, no. They'd been friends, though, or so he'd thought. Or, no, possibly friends wasn't quite the right way to think about it, since he had friends and the way he felt about them was *not* how he felt about Lia.

He'd wanted her, been desperate for her. Had been obsessed with her. He knew he shouldn't have kept wandering past her father's study every night, but somehow that's where his path had always seemed to take him no matter his intentions.

Those nights he'd spent sipping whisky and discussing everything under the sun with her, from politics to philosophy, science and the arts, social theory and everything in between.

Those nights where he'd realised he wanted her more than he'd wanted anyone or anything in his entire life and the fury he'd felt because she would *never* be his. She'd always been destined for Matias and for Santa Castelia.

*She isn't now, though. Now, she can be yours.*

The possessive heat he'd been trying to keep at bay for the past three months poured suddenly through him in a searing flood, as if a dam had broken.

Because it was true, wasn't it? He'd told her that she had to marry him, not fully thinking about what that would mean.

Her, in his bed. Her, whenever he wanted her.

He wouldn't have to constantly watch himself whenever he was around her in case he gave himself away. He wouldn't have to constantly fight his own intense desire for her or the jealousy that gripped him whenever he thought about her with Matias.

She would be his.

Possessiveness caught him by the throat, but he choked it down with an instinct he'd spent most of his life perfecting.

His emotions were too intense, too potent to allow free rein. Hadn't his mother told him often enough that he had to be careful? That he had to control himself if he didn't want to turn into his father? The only reason he hadn't yet done so was because he wouldn't permit himself off the leash.

Lia was a danger to that control, it was true, but marriage might help. It was likely she'd got under his skin so badly because of the forbidden element in their relationship and since that wasn't a problem any more, he'd likely obsess about her less.

Knowing he'd be a father, too, was its own leash.

His own father had been morally bankrupt and Rafael would *not* set that kind of example. No, the family he'd create would be different.

*And Matias? Santa Castelia?*

Yes, those two things were yet more reasons why marriage was the only answer. He had to set an example for his brother and for the country he ruled. He had to show them that taking responsibility for your mistakes was the only way forward.

Anton was still standing there, looking apologetic, so Rafael dismissed him.

Constanza, his housekeeper, appeared at the door, also looking apologetic. 'There have been calls, Excellency.' She paused, then added, 'Many calls.'

Naturally.

'From His Highness?' Rafael asked.

Constanza inclined her head. 'And from the First Advisor. Not to mention from Their Highnesses Prince Zeus and Prince Jahangir

Hassan Umar Al Hayat, and His Royal Majesty the King of Arista.'

Rafael gritted his teeth. Naturally his three Oxford friends would know what he'd done and have something to say about it. The news media would no doubt be buzzing.

They could wait, though. Before he talked to anyone else, he had to get Lia's agreement to their marriage, because forcing it from her was a path he'd never go down.

*You didn't find her agreement necessary when you kidnapped her from the cathedral.*

Yes, and that was because he'd allowed his emotions to get the better of him. A good reminder of why he had to stay in control.

He was too dangerous otherwise.

'Tell anyone who calls that the Princess Amalia is well and that we will be releasing a statement shortly,' he ordered. 'Then see that the Mountain Suite is made ready. Also prepare some immediate refreshments suitable for a pregnant woman. We will also be dining in the formal dining room tonight. The food must be exquisite, understand?' He thought a moment. 'The Princess also needs a change of clothes. See what you can find for her.'

Constanza, who was very rarely flustered, inclined her head again. 'Certainly, Excellency.'

Rafael thought a little more. 'Are there any staff here ordained?'

She remained unflustered. 'No, Excellency. I am the only staff member here and unfortunately I cannot help you.'

Well, that would be an issue he'd deal with later if and when it arose.

Rafael dismissed the housekeeper, then turned and strode back down the hallway to the living area where he'd left Lia.

She was still sitting on the couch before the fire. Her face was pale and she looked… tired. Sympathy tightened in his chest and this time he let it.

His mother had been a maid at the five-star hotel in Barcelona that his father preferred whenever he visited Spain. She'd been beautiful and he smitten. He was a king, used to taking what he wanted and so he'd taken her. And Rafael was the consequence. He'd been her burden to bear, not his father's, and borne him she had, on her own.

He couldn't allow the same thing to happen to Lia. He wouldn't leave her to do this alone. That was not the example he wanted to set.

She looked up as he entered, her eyes widening. 'I thought we were going to discuss this later?'

'We were.' He came to a stop in front of the fire, holding his hands out to the flames, letting them warm the chilled tips of his fingers. 'But it appears that the roads are blocked. No one can get in or out.'

'I see.' Her voice was very neutral.

He almost smiled. She always sounded like that when she disagreed with people—in public at least. In private, neutral was the last thing she was.

'Which means, *princesa,*' he said, 'that you and I will have our little discussion now.'

'Do we need to have a discussion? I'm not marrying you, Rafael.'

Of course, getting her agreement wasn't going to be simple. He couldn't say that he hadn't hoped, but this was Lia after all. She was a complicated woman.

He wasn't displeased with the notion of having to work for it, however. He'd always loved it when she argued with him, because so very few people did. Plus, she challenged him and he did so love a challenge.

Slowly, he turned from the fire and faced her.

She was composed, as if the woman who'd thrown her bouquet and tried to hit him had never existed. Her diamond circlet was now on straight, her veil draped decorously back from her hair, her long-fingered, elegant hands folded in her lap.

The picture-perfect Crown Princess.

Except for the wet fabric that clung to her ankles and the water stains that sprinkled the expensive white silk.

'Why not?' He kept his tone as neutral as hers, as if they were having a discussion about what kind of food they'd like for dinner or what drink they preferred. 'You are pregnant with my child.'

'Believe it or not, I'm well aware of that.'

Her inky lashes fell as she looked down at her hands. 'However, marrying me just because I'm pregnant is not the most compelling of proposals.'

'And what would constitute a compelling proposal? Is it money you're after? Power? You said you didn't want to let your parents down and, if so, perhaps they would be satisfied with you having a high-powered executive position in one of my companies?'

She shook her head. 'No. I just…don't want to marry anyone who feels forced into marrying me.'

He stared at her, not understanding. 'How is that any different from marrying Matias? You've been betrothed since you were children.'

She kept her gaze on her hands and stayed silent.

His temper pulled at the leash, along with his hunger and that possessiveness he couldn't seem to lock away. 'You know what people call me. "The Spanish Bastard".' He said the words with a certain relish, watching her face. 'It is not a compliment, *princesa*. And let me be clear, I don't care. It doesn't bother me. But I will not leave my child open to such names or such contempt. And if you're expecting to be sent out of the country to live in exile somewhere with a nice stipend, you will be very disappointed.'

He put his hands in his pockets and took a leisurely step towards her. 'Some day, at some point, no matter how hard you hide it, someone will discover that I am the father of that child. And when they do, you will find the media camped on your doorstep. You will have no rest. They will hound you.' He took another step towards her. 'And they will hound our child, too. Your reputation will be called into question, because the press are always hard on women. Every aspect of your life will be picked over.' Another step. 'Matias will be made to look a fool. The crown will be embarrassed and everyone will say "Like father, like son". Santa Castelia will be the laughing stock of the entire world.'

She kept her gaze down, but her jaw became very set.

He stopped in front of her, the tips of his expensive, hand-made black leather shoes grazing the white spill of wet silk from her skirts. 'So, tell me, Lia. Is that a more compelling proposal?'

# CHAPTER FOUR

RAFAEL STOOD IN front of her, the tips of his shoes brushing her gown, tall and dark, muscular. Towering over her.

She kept her attention on her hands, but she could feel him watching her. His barely contained sense of frustration was almost palpable.

He'd always hated it when people didn't give in to his wishes and he clearly thought she should. Then again, she'd had some time to think, sitting out here in front of the fire, and she'd come to a few decisions.

The future she'd always thought she was destined for had been ripped away from her and, yes, that had been her fault. Her parents were going to be so disappointed and so was Matias, not to mention Santa Castelia, but there was no hope of her regaining the position she'd once had.

That was gone, as Rafael had so clearly laid out just now.

Which meant that for the first time in her life, Lia was faced with a choice about what she wanted.

She didn't have to be Queen.

She didn't have to rule a nation.

She didn't have to marry a man she didn't love.

She didn't have to be the Crown Princess.

The only thing she had to be was a mother and, though providing heirs had always been another thing that was expected of her, she didn't have to raise them to be royal as she had been.

She could be the kind of mother *she* wanted to be. She could do the things *she* wanted to do.

And there was no one to disappoint, not when she'd disappointed everyone already.

She'd never had that before. She'd never even thought about it.

What this would mean for herself and her child she didn't know. But one thing she *was* sure of: Matias hadn't ever said anything to her openly, but she'd always had the impression that she wasn't his choice. That he was marrying her purely for duty's sake and not because he actually liked spending time with her.

She'd tried not to let that bother her, but it did. And since she was being given the choice, she didn't want that now.

For once in her life, she wanted to be someone who was chosen and not for what she could bring or for what she represented, but for herself.

But Rafael hadn't chosen her. He was only marrying her because her pregnancy had forced his hand. And she didn't want that.

She didn't want to be someone's duty or their fix, or their reluctant consequence. And she especially didn't want to be Rafael's.

So, no, she wasn't going to marry him, no matter how many reasons he gave her as to why she should.

Oh, they were good reasons, she understood that. But none of them necessitated actual marriage. Besides, she was tired of doing what everyone else wanted her to do.

Why shouldn't she get what she wanted for a change?

'No,' she said flatly and at last lifted her gaze to his. 'That is not compelling in the slightest.'

It was hard to hold his intense stare, but she managed it. Giving him back as good as she got, the way she always had in the arguments they'd had with each other. Studying the harsh planes and angles of his face, so hard and uncompromising.

Her heart fluttered in her chest in the confusing way it always did whenever she was around him.

'Then what, *princesa?*' A muscle jumped in the side of his jaw. 'Shall I get down on one knee? Is that what you want?'

'No.' She had nothing but the truth to give him. 'I want to be chosen, Rafael. I want someone to marry me because they want *me*. Not because they have no other choice or because our parents arranged it. I'm tired of being someone's duty and I don't want to be someone's obligation.'

His intense gaze narrowed. 'You're not an obligation.'

'Aren't I? You're only marrying me because I'm pregnant.'

'So? This wouldn't even be an option if you weren't, because you'd be marrying Matias.'

'Exactly. But I don't have to do that now.' She lifted her chin, held his hard stare. 'Which means I can choose for myself for a change.'

His expression didn't alter, but that muscle jumped in his jaw again, the sense of contained frustration gathering tighter in the room.

It was clear that he did *not* like this decision one bit.

'And what about our child?' His dark, harsh voice was gritty with temper. 'It's not just about you and your choices.'

Her own temper rose as it always did when matched with his, the inevitable excitement she felt whenever she was around him rising, too.

She'd told herself she was going to be calm and measured, but she'd got to her feet before she could stop herself. 'Your whole life has been about what you want, Rafael. All the choices you've made have been for yourself. But mine haven't. Right from the moment I could walk I've been told what my future is, what role I have to take. No one ever asked me what I wanted. Everything was *always* chosen for me.'

Rafael's features hardened. 'Yes, and as I told you before, *you* could have chosen differently. No one was forcing you into marrying Matias.'

*He's right and you know it.*

Lia ignored the thought. 'Don't be ridiculous. I had to marry him. You think I could just go and tell him I'd changed my mind? That I could tell my parents that all the work they'd put organising the betrothal and all the training I was given—'

'All that work that no one asked them to do,' he snapped. 'It was what *they* wanted, Lia. You said yourself that no one ever asked you what you wanted. They didn't even think about you.' His gaze glittered. 'So why nail yourself to a cross you didn't even build?'

Her stomach hollowed, a cold feeling winding through her.

*You told yourself all this time that they were doing this for you. But was that really the case?*

Even as a little girl, no one had asked her what she wanted to be when she grew up. And no one asked because everyone knew exactly what Lia would be when she grew up.

Matias's wife. The Queen.

But it had never been a choice, no matter what he said.

*Except what if you had said no?*

Lia shoved that thought away. She was tired and she didn't want to talk about this any more. 'We've had our discussion,' she said evenly, trying not to give in to her temper. 'I've told you why I don't want to marry you. I'm not sure why you're arguing with me about it, but I suppose it's because you hate it when people don't do exactly what you want.'

'That's not—'

'I'm tired, I'm cold and I don't want to continue this discussion.' She kept her tone firm. 'There's no more to be said.'

Rafael was silent a long moment, his relentless silver gaze boring into her.

She stared back, refusing to be cowed.

She was younger than he, less experienced than he and had no power to speak of, but none of that mattered.

Her will was as strong as his and they both knew it.

Tension gathered between them, drawing tighter and tighter.

Her breath caught, every part of her suddenly coming alive. Aware of him on the most basic level, of his height, his heat and his sheer masculine power.

He could make her do anything he wanted. He could use that power, that strength to bend her to his will. Yet he never had and she knew he never would—that was why she felt no fear as she faced into the storm force of his displeasure. She'd never been afraid of him even when everyone else had…

*Lia stood beside some of the other palace staff on one of the balconies that overlooked the grand front stairs of the palace, all of them craning for a glimpse of the infamous new Regent.*

*Her father and Matias were among the delegation waiting on the steps, all attention on the long black limo that had pulled up in front. The door opened.*

*A man got out. He was so tall, taller than even the Prince, who towered over most. He was dressed in an expensive and perfectly tailored dark suit with a black shirt underneath and, the moment he straightened up, everyone fell silent. He wasn't handsome like some of her favourite actors, or pretty like her boy-band crushes, yet all the same he was the most compelling man Lia had ever seen in all her seventeen years.*

*There was something about him that drew her, that fascinated her. Something to do with the natural power and authority he radiated, a man in complete control of himself and the world he lived in. A man utterly unlike his father, King Carlos, who'd been unpredictable, wild and corrupt. No one wanted another king like that and everyone was afraid that the decision to bring in King Carlos's illegitimate son to rule until Matias was of age had been a bad one.*

*Lia could hear people whispering and knew they were afraid as they stared at the man they called the 'Spanish Bastard', a financial genius and CEO of one of the world's biggest finance companies.*

*It had been Lia's father's decision to ask Rafael Navarro to rule Santa Castelia as Prince Regent, in the hope that he would be able to restore a decimated treasury and guide the Prince on a better path than the one their father had walked.*

*Others had opposed the decision and, looking at the man striding up the steps of the palace as if he owned it already, Lia could understand their fear.*

*But she knew—and how she knew she had no idea, she just did—that they had nothing to be afraid of. This man was not Carlos. In fact, Lia's almost bone-deep instinct was that he was the opposite. Strong where Carlos had been weak. Steady where Carlos had been unpredictable. Calm where Carlos had been wild and cool where Carlos had been hot.*

*This man would heal Santa Castelia, she just knew it.*

*At the top of the grand stairs, Rafael Navarro turned to address the assembled crowd. He had the most extraordinary eyes, a light grey that glittered like silver, in stark contrast to his black hair and brows.*

*He leisurely took in everyone that stood before him, as if acknowledging each and every one of them, even those on the balconies. And when that silver gaze came to her, she felt an answering pulse deep inside, as if part of her knew exactly what he would eventually come to mean to her...*

'Well,' he said at last, his casual tone so at odds with that blazing silver gaze she knew so intimately, 'I can see that this might take some time. Then again, we do have the whole night.' He glanced down at the hideously expensive watch that circled one strong wrist.

'Constanza will have prepared the Mountain Suite for you and a change of clothes, so you can get warm at least. I've also ordered some refreshments to be brought. Perhaps some time to change and something to eat will help you feel better.'

'Feel better meaning change my mind?'

Strangely, something that looked like reluctant amusement rippled over his harsh features, gone so fast she wasn't sure she'd seen it at all. Reminding her that it hadn't all been fiery intellectual arguments and challenges. He had a very dry sense of humour that rarely showed itself, but when it did, when she'd managed to make him smile, she'd always felt as if she'd won a lottery.

That same rush of warmth sparked inside her now, lighting her up inside.

'You never know,' he murmured. 'What about if I added some whisky and cigars?'

The warmth expanded. Whisky and cigars, and Rafael's exciting, vital presence. The bright points in a life that had been far more curtailed than she ever let herself think too deeply about.

She'd missed him. She'd missed him so much.

'Sadly,' she said, 'I don't think the baby would like it.'

The lines around his hard mouth eased, that elusive spark of humour glowing briefly in his eyes. 'True enough.'

Their gazes met again and held. This time it wasn't the clash of their wills that held her still, but something else. Something aching and raw and painful.

The signs of humour in Rafael's face vanished, leaving behind it a familiar heat that stole all the breath from her body. Three months ago, when she'd still been the sheltered girl he'd accused her of being, she hadn't recognised that heat for what it was. But she did now. Oh, she did now.

Desire.

'Your gown is wet.' He didn't look away, the harsh gravel of his voice becoming suddenly rough velvet. 'Let me help you with it.'

Her mouth had gone dry, her heart beating

hard and fast in her ears. He was looking at her as though he wanted to eat her alive and, God help her, she wanted him to.

If anything could make her change her mind about marrying him, it wasn't money or power, or even warm clothes and good food.

It was him. It was his touch.

'I'm fine.' Her voice sounded almost as low as his.

'But you can't undo all those buttons yourself.'

Heat prickled everywhere, chasing away the cold, bringing with it a heady rush of excitement.

She couldn't drag her gaze from his, every part of her consumed with the sudden, intense need to close the distance between them. To end the nagging hunger they both felt.

It had always been this way with him. Whenever he was near, she'd been almost overtaken by this fierce craving for him. It had been an unfamiliar and alien feeling that before their night together she hadn't understood.

She did now, though. It was powerful sexual desire.

She wanted him to touch her, kiss her, be inside her.

She wanted him so badly she couldn't breathe.

But sex had created this problem, which meant that more sex was hardly the solution. She had to control herself and not give in. Put more distance between them not less.

'I'll manage,' she forced out.

The heat in his eyes nearly burned her alive, but he didn't move. Then his gaze shifted. 'Ah, Constanza. Please show the Crown Princess to the Mountain Suite. I assume you have found appropriate clothing for her to wear?'

Behind Lia, a woman said in low tones, 'Yes, Excellency.'

'Good.' His hard mouth curved slightly as his gaze shifted back to her, but there was no amusement in it this time. It was the half-feral smile of a starving tiger who'd just sighted prey. 'Turn around, *princesa*. You do not want to ruin that gown and you will if you're not careful. Constanza would help, but she has bad arthritis and those buttons are very small.'

Ah, God, this was a challenge wasn't it? And she'd never been able to resist the challenges he'd thrown at her...

*Don't forget that the power isn't all with him. You have that same power, too.*

Another thing she wouldn't have understood three months ago, if she hadn't been in his bed.

But she had and she knew that the same desire she felt for him, he also felt for her and that she could use it. She could tempt him every bit as much as he was tempting her.

It wasn't the wisest course of action right now, not when she'd already decided to maintain her distance from him, not get closer. But he'd kidnapped her from her own wedding. She was trapped in his house and he was trying to make her marry him and really, if she wanted to get brutal about it, he was also using their baby to manipulate her.

It was time to turn the tables.

Hunger gleamed in his eyes and a dizzying excitement caught at her. She'd never had the opportunity to flirt with him like this. To tease him, tempt him. She'd been too innocent before.

Yet she wasn't innocent now and there was nothing to stop them, so why not?

It didn't mean giving in. All it meant was giving him a taste of his own medicine.

'In that case,' she said huskily and turned around, presenting her back to him, 'you may deal with the buttons.'

The older woman she'd seen before stood in the doorway. Constanza, apparently. The woman inclined her head in response to some unspoken command and vanished back down the hall, leaving as silently as she came.

The only sound in the room was the crackle of the flames in the fireplace and the frantic beat of her pulse.

Rafael was standing close, but not too close. Enough to feel the intense heat of his body and smell his familiar scent.

Her chest tightened, her throat closing.

His fingers tugged gently on the first button, a delicious tension gathering deep inside her, along with a bone-deep longing.

It was the same tension she'd felt whenever Rafael strode in and sat in the chair on the other side of the desk. Whenever his silver gaze met hers.

Was he thinking about that right now? Had he felt that same tension? That same longing?

He'd never said anything openly, never mentioned the thick atmosphere that used to fill her father's study sometimes when he looked at her.

The first time she'd known that their attraction was mutual had been when he'd unleashed that storm of passion the night she'd spent in his arms.

He said nothing now as he began to undo all the buttons, his fingers deft and sure, the fabric parting, cool air drifting over her bared skin.

She remembered this. Remembered being naked with him, feeling the touch of his hands and the brush of his mouth, the heat of his hard, muscular body on hers. The strength of his arms, gathering her close...

Did he remember this, too? Did he long for it as she did?

Perhaps he didn't. Perhaps she was seeing things in his expression, in his gaze, that weren't there. Perhaps it was all in her head.

Whatever, this was a mistake. She had to stop letting her stupid emotions control her.

Lia swallowed, her throat bone dry, preparing to pull away.

Then he said quietly, 'Ah, yes. I remember this view.'

In the silence of the room, Rafael heard her breath catch.

She was warm and she smelled of the honeysuckle that grew on the stone walls in the older part of the palace. Light, sweet, delicious...

He shouldn't be doing this, not when she tested his control so completely, but she'd been adamant, refusing to listen to all good sense and logic about marrying him. Insisting on wanting to be chosen for herself and not because he'd been 'forced' into it.

He understood her protests, at least intellectually. She'd been chosen for Matias. Matias hadn't chosen her. He hadn't been passionate about her. He'd found her dull. She was a duty and if Rafael had taught him nothing else, it was that doing one's duty was imperative.

And it was true that she'd never been given the opportunity to choose for herself what she wanted out of life. Then again, she was an adult woman, full of fire and spirit, and she could have refused the path her parents had laid out for her. And he didn't understand why she hadn't.

He'd wanted to press her about that, but once Lia didn't want to talk about something, she didn't want to talk. She was stubborn like that.

Just as she was stubborn about refusing to marry him.

Using their chemistry to remind her that there would be some compensations to being his wife was perhaps manipulative, but when it came to the wellbeing of his child there was nothing he wouldn't do.

Anyway, if she wanted to be chosen, then he would choose her. Because while it was true that if she hadn't fallen pregnant, he would never have even contemplated marrying her, the fact that no other woman tempted him the way she did hadn't changed.

He'd never wanted to marry, but the more he thought about having Lia as his wife, the more attractive the idea became. Being married to her would certainly be no hardship and definitely not any kind of duty.

He just had to convince her of that.

The fabric of her gown had parted, revealing the elegant curve of her spine, all pale skin and softness.

Desire kicked hard inside him, stealing his breath.

'How could you remember?' She didn't ask him what he was talking about. She knew. 'It was dark.'

The fire crackled, painting her exposed back in shades of rose and gold, and he wanted to touch her, brush his fingers down her back, feel the warm satin of her skin.

'Not completely.' His heart was beating far too fast, the need to touch her almost uncontrollable. He curled his fingers into fists, dug his nails into his palms, trying to master himself. 'There was a gap in the curtains and the moon shone through it.'

The moon had made her look as though she was carved out of ice and snow that night. Yet she hadn't been a snow queen. No, she'd been made of fire…

*Moonlight outlined the delectable curves of the woman lying in his arms, her back to his chest. She had her head turned away, her cheek pressed to the pillow and she was shivering with desire. His hand traced her side, the dip of her waist and the achingly beautiful curve of her hip. She was so warm, so soft.*

*He'd had so many illicit fantasies about her and she was everything those fantasies had promised. No, she was more. She was better…*

*This was wrong and he knew it, and continuing to do this with her when his instinct was screaming at him to stop was insanity. A betrayal of everything he'd told himself he was. Everything he'd worked for up to this point.*

*But the desire she'd unleashed in him was impossible to deny.*

*'Rafael,' she murmured, arching against him, his name a prayer and a plea.*

*And he was lost, his control in ashes.*

*She had come to* him. *She had begged for* him. *She had risked everything to have one night with him and he would fight God himself if he tried to take her from him.*

*She wanted* him. *Not because he was the Regent, not for his power or his authority or the money in his bank account. Him. Not his brother, the heir, the Crown Prince.*

*She wanted the Spanish bastard who'd grown up in a rundown one-bedroom apartment in Barcelona. Whom nobody had wanted, not his father and certainly not his mother.*

*This night between them should never had happened, but he was going to take it. No one would know. No one would ever find out.*

*It would remain their secret.*

*He ran his hand down her side, her skin feeling like warm satin, and she sighed, trembling with delight...*

\* \* \*

'You said you were angry when you came looking for Matias that night,' he heard himself say, his hand half lifting to brush the nape of her neck despite himself. 'What were you angry about?'

She was silent for a long moment and he thought she wouldn't answer. Then she said, her voice husky, 'I was…angry with you for making me want you. And angry with myself. I couldn't stop thinking about you, I couldn't… I was supposed to be marrying your brother and I wanted you out of my head.' She took a little breath. 'I thought Matias would help me forget you and I suppose there was a part of me that wanted to punish you.'

A hot, primitive sense of satisfaction gripped him, a strange feeling, tangled as it was with anger and possessiveness and jealousy.

Satisfaction that she wanted him so much she hadn't been able to stop thinking about him. Anger and possessiveness and jealousy that she'd wanted to punish him with Matias.

'I didn't know what else to do,' she went on, as if once she'd decided to talk, she couldn't stop. 'The betrothal ball was the next day and you'd stopped turning up to our meetings. And I didn't know why. And I—'

'You know why,' he interrupted. 'I stopped turning up because every night was a constant battle against the urge to touch you. And I was losing.'

She stood so very still, tense in every line. Her breathing was audible and fast, though he could also hear her trying to control it. 'You were losing?'

He stared at her straight back, at the soft vulnerability of her nape left bare by the ornate curls her black hair had been arranged in.

She had been so sheltered, so innocent. She'd had no idea about sexual chemistry or desire, and he hadn't wanted her to have to deal with his. What he'd felt for her was so wrong and the only thing he could do about it was to take himself out of her vicinity.

So that's what he'd done.

'Yes.' Telling her this was a mistake, but she'd given him a little piece of truth just before and it didn't seem fair not to reciprocate. 'I wanted you more than I'd wanted anything in my entire life. But you were meant for Matias and so I stopped coming. It was easier.'

There was complete silence in the room broken only by the crackle of the fire in the grate.

He wanted to touch her so badly his chest ached.

She turned, her pale face flushed, a blue flame burning in her eyes.

*Dios*, but she was beautiful when she wasn't the good, quiet, delicate Crown Princess that Matias had found so dull, when she was the hot, passionate woman. The woman who wanted him every bit as badly as he wanted her.

'I thought you'd stopped coming because you'd lost interest.' She searched his face as if he held all the answers to every question she'd ever had. 'I didn't think…' She stopped, the flush in her cheeks deepening, the blue flame in her eyes glowing brighter.

*You could take her now. Right here in front of the fire.*

He could and she wouldn't resist him, he could see that right now. But the need inside him felt too big and too strong. Something that he should resist, not give in to. Especially when he knew himself and his desires. They were powerful and, if he wasn't careful, if he wasn't vigilant, he could fall prey to them like his father had.

His mother had been clear about the dangers when he'd been a child and he'd never forgotten those lessons. He couldn't afford to. And if he needed a reminder, he only had to look at the woman in front of him.

A woman he'd taken without any thought for her and her future. Who was now pregnant and alone, just as his mother had been.

No, he couldn't let himself be at the mercy of his own desires, not now, not when his control was so tenuous. He had lost so many battles since meeting her, but he would not lose this one.

He held her bright gaze, freezing every part of the fire that leapt inside him. 'Constanza will have prepared your suite by now,' he said, keeping his tone casual. 'Perhaps you would like to change your gown and refresh yourself.'

Lia took an impulsive step towards him. 'But I—'

'It was not a request, *princesa*.' He held himself still, ignoring the warmth of her that lapped around him, tugging at him. She needed to be out of his vicinity and quickly.

Uncurling his fingers with a certain deliberation, he lifted his hand and instantly Constanza reappeared. 'Show the Lady Amalia to her suite, please.'

Lia stared at him a long moment, then abruptly her lashes lowered, veiling the glow in her eyes. 'Yes,' she said. 'Now that you mention it, perhaps that would be for the best.'

She didn't say anything more, turning and following Constanza, shoulders back, her chin held high, sweeping from the room in a cloud of silken skirts. It would have been dignified if her gown hadn't been almost fully open at the back and only on her shoulders because she was holding it there.

Rafael watched her leave, standing rigid until she'd gone, before turning back to the fire and getting a grip on his recalcitrant body.

If he wanted to try that tactic again, use their chemistry to get her to do what he wanted, then he was going to have to be very careful. That was a flame that could easily burn out of control if he let it.

His phone went off and he pulled it out of his jacket pocket, answering it absently, his head still full of Lia.

'What the hell are you doing?' a deep voice said in his ear.

Zeus. One of his three closest friends and the one least likely to judge Rafael's current behaviour. Which wasn't a point in his favour.

Why on earth had he answered his phone?

'Is there a point to this call, Zeus?' He kept his tone negligent as he stared into the flames. 'Because if not, my hands are rather full right now.'

'A point? Not at all. But I've had Vincenzo

and Jag yelling in my ear for the past hour and I'm sick of it. Why aren't you answering our calls?'

'I would have thought that would be obvious.'

'You took your brother's bride right from under his nose,' Zeus said. 'You just threw her over your shoulder in full view of everyone. I have to say, I'm impressed. I didn't think you had it in you.'

Rafael gritted his teeth. He'd always been the most restrained of the four, while Zeus wouldn't know restraint if it punched him in the face. 'She's pregnant,' he growled. 'What was I supposed to do?'

'Pregnant?' Zeus sounded surprised this time. 'Rafael, did you—?'

'Yes,' he interrupted. 'The child is mine.' And then, because this was an old friend after all, he added, 'It's complicated.'

'Apparently.' Zeus's tone was dry as dust. 'So, what are you going to do now?'

'What do you think I'm going to do now? I'm going to marry her.'

'Oh, good.' This time Zeus did not sound in the least bit surprised. 'I'll get the jet ready.'

'No,' Rafael said. 'It's a white out. All the roads are blocked and no one can get in or out.'

'Well, that's disappointing. I was looking forward to marrying another of my friends. How is the prospective bride?'

'Very angry.'

Zeus laughed. 'I see. She wasn't happy with being thrown over your shoulder, I take it?'

'She wasn't.'

'She'd rather be with your brother then?'

*I wanted you... I couldn't stop thinking about you...'*

'No.' Rafael was unable to keep the satisfaction from his voice. 'She doesn't. She's angry because she doesn't like being told what to do.'

'I can relate.'

'But that child is my responsibility and so I'm taking it.'

'Indeed. Vincenzo and Jag will be relieved to hear it wasn't just you losing your mind.'

'Their concern is noted.'

'What about Matias and the rest of your country?'

Trust Zeus to ask the most uncomfortable question.

'What about them?' He didn't bother with any politeness, not that his old friend would expect it anyway.

Zeus paused, then said delicately, 'Considering she was supposed to be Matias's bride and Santa Castelia's Queen...'

Rafael's jaw clenched. 'I told you. She felt nothing for Matias and he felt nothing for her. And as for Santa Castelia, another queen can be found.'

'But wasn't she brought up specifically for the role?'

Another uncomfortable question. Rafael was tired of them. 'Did you have anything else you wanted to say?' he demanded.

'You didn't answer my—'

'Good.' Rafael hit the end button and got rid of the call.

Then after a second's thought, he turned his phone off.

He didn't want any distractions and he most

especially didn't want anyone questioning what he'd done in that cathedral. It made him think about all the lines he'd crossed, all the vows he'd broken.

Vows he'd made to Santa Castelia and to his brother.

Vows he'd made to himself.

He'd sworn the day he'd learned the truth about his father that he'd never let his anger rule him again. He'd never let *any* emotion rule him. And he would never allow another woman to go through what his mother had.

His birth had been a mistake and he had had to make up for that, channelling all the heat of his violent emotions into a cold, driving will that had taken him out of that one-roomed apartment in Barcelona and turned him into the man he was today.

The owner of a global company, ruler of an entire nation. Mentor to a king…

*Matias had their father's height and his dark colouring, though his eyes weren't as dark as Carlos's had been. They looked at Rafael warily now as the last of the advisors filed out of the meeting room. Rafael had ordered them out for some privacy.*

*Matias, sixteen, yet looking even younger, didn't say a word. He stared at Rafael as if he was a rabid dog that might bite at any moment.*

*He was scared, Rafael got that loud and clear, and it made the low, sullen anger that burned constantly inside him leap. Carlos had not been kind to him, that was clear. If their father had hurt him...*

*Rafael gritted his teeth and forced his fury down, meeting his brother's gaze directly. 'First of all,' he said, 'I am not here to take your place. My duty is to get Santa Castelia into shape so that you actually have a country to rule and not a dictator's republic. Second, although I will make the ultimate decisions on how this country is run, I aim to involve you in all the decision-making processes. You need to be taught how to rule and, since our father neglected his duty and failed to teach you, I will do so.'*

*The boy remained quiet, still staring.*

*'Third, you are the Crown Prince and I am*

*here to protect your interests. Everything I do here, I do for you. Do you understand?'*

*Matias continued to stare for so long that Rafael wondered if the boy would ever talk. Then finally he said, 'Why? Why did you say yes?'*

*Rafael knew what he was asking and it was the same question he'd asked himself when Gian De Vita had called him out of the blue not long after the news of his father's death had broken, asking him if he would consider ruling Santa Castelia.*

*'I said yes, because someone had to do it. Because I am not our father and I didn't want the crown. And because someone had to teach you the right way to be King.'*

*There was anger in Matias's gaze, though whether it was for him or something else, Rafael couldn't tell. 'Why not Gian? He could have been Regent.'*

*'Santa Castelia needs money. And Gian doesn't have the financial understanding that I do.' He paused. 'Are you angry with me?'*

*There was a silence, then Matias said sud-*

*denly, 'He always liked you better. He said I was weak.'*

*Rafael didn't need to ask who Matias meant. It was obvious.*

*'Well,' he replied mildly, 'let's prove him wrong.'*

And they had. They both had. Matias had grown into his strength, gaining a quiet sort of confidence and authority that wasn't Rafael's hard edge, but had a power of its own.

*And by taking Lia, you've undermined everything you tried to build. And you thought you were nothing like your father...*

Bitterness coiled inside him, but he shoved it down.

He *wasn't* anything like his father. At least Rafael acknowledged his own mistakes and took ownership of them.

Not that his child was a mistake. Never that.

'Your Excellency,' Constanza said from the doorway. 'Your Highness, your brother is calling. Do you wish to speak with him?'

'No,' Rafael said, staring down into the fire. 'Tell him I cannot be contacted.'

First, he would fix things with Lia.

Then, he would confront his brother.

# CHAPTER FIVE

LIA KEPT HER back straight and her chin held high all the way up the stairs that led to the second floor of the house and all the way down a wide hallway with discreet recessed lighting and low ceilings. She didn't falter as Constanza stopped outside a door of dark wood and opened it, gesturing her inside. She simply inclined her head in thanks and swept into the room.

It was only when the door had closed quietly behind her and she was alone that she gave in to the trembling that shook her entire body.

She was aware of every inch of her exposed back, of how flimsy the hold of the fabric on her shoulders was and how easily it could slip. Downstairs, all she'd had to do was shrug slightly and her gown would have fallen into a pool of silken tulle and lace at her feet.

She would have been naked but for her white silk lacy underwear.

What would he have done then? Would he have touched her? And if he had, what would she have done in return?

'*...every night was a constant battle against the urge to touch you. And I was losing...*'

She shut her eyes, feeling again the gentle tug on the buttons of her gown and the warmth of him at her back. So close, so achingly close.

That's why he hadn't come to any more of their nightly meetings. '*I wanted you more than I'd wanted anything in my entire life.*'

She might have been sheltered, but she'd recognised his desire for her. She'd known. But to hear him say it out loud...

The stern, controlled Regent, so cold and so commanding, had wanted her, had burned for her...

'*You're just like my father sometimes,*' *she snapped, unable to help herself.* '*So damn patronising. Are you even listening to what I'm saying? Or is it because I'm a sheltered young woman you don't think I know anything?'*

*Rafael was in his customary pose, sitting back in the chair opposite the desk, his long, muscular body stretched out, ankles crossed. Ostensibly relaxed and yet tonight something was different. There was a tension about him that needled her, that stretched her own temper thin and she wasn't sure why.*

*Silver glittered in his eyes. He seemed cold tonight, the distance between them and their respective stations making the desk seem like an impossible gulf.*

*'No,' he said and she could hear anger in his voice. 'I do not think that.'*

*Her emotions had always moved liked quicksilver and her anger faded as quickly as it had come, because something was wrong, she could sense it.*

*She frowned. 'Is everything all right, Rafael?'*

*His gaze flickered. 'Yes. Why do you ask?'*

*'Because you're not usually this grumpy.'*

*He shifted in his chair, the tension around him gathering tighter. 'There have been... some issues I have to deal with.'*

*'I'm sorry. Is there anything I can—?'*

*'You are a sheltered young woman,' he interrupted suddenly. 'And there are some things you don't know anything about.'*

*An intensity vibrated suddenly in his voice, a rough quality that made her go very still, her heart thudding hard in her head.*

*'What things?' she asked, staring at him, her breath catching.*

*He looked back and for a long time neither of them moved, the air in the study aromatic with the remains of her cigar and the warm scent of Rafael's aftershave drifting around her.*

*There was heat in his eyes, making her skin prickle everywhere.*

*Then abruptly he cursed, put down his tumbler of Scotch, pushed himself violently to his feet and walked out.*

Lia swallowed, her head full of the look in his eyes as she'd turned to him downstairs.

She'd wanted to see his face, wanted to see the truth and there it had been, that same look he'd given her that night months ago, his silver gaze full of desire. For her.

*What if you weren't meant for Matias after all? What if you were meant for him?*

Her heart was beating far too fast and she felt breathless.

Meant for him, for Rafael…

The idea made everything in her pull taut.

Ever since she'd first seen him on the balcony all those years ago, he'd generated such a strong response inside her. Back then she'd only been seventeen and sheltered, and hadn't known what it meant. He'd fascinated her, confused her, but even then part of her had known that the feelings she had for him were forbidden. That they should have been for Matias, not Rafael.

Her parents had ensured she spent time with Matias, organising decently chaperoned outings so the two of them could get to know one another. But he'd never seemed to display much interest in her. Their conversations had been stilted and awkward, both of them running out of things to say to each other.

She'd thought it would get easier between them, that they merely needed more time, but then those meetings with Rafael had happened and she'd become even more confused. Because conversation with Rafael had never been awkward or stilted. He'd never seemed bored by what she had to say and, unlike Matias, he was interested in her opinions.

She loved talking to him, loved spending time with him, and the more evenings she had with him, the more she wanted. She'd started resenting having to go on outings with Matias and on the days she did, all she could think about was that she didn't have these long silences with Rafael. And she didn't have to watch what she said with Rafael or be the perfect princess with Rafael.

She didn't feel the same heady combination of excited and afraid that she felt when she was with Rafael, that she *only* felt with Rafael…

*It wasn't only physical desire you felt for him.*
But her mind shied away from that thought.

It felt too big, too dangerous. A teenage crush was far more manageable and really, that's exactly what it had been. A teenage crush she hadn't grown out of and a physical desire she hadn't managed to control.

Except she would control it now, because she had choices now and a future that hadn't been planned in meticulous detail for her by other people. She had decisions to make and she couldn't let those decisions be dictated by some emotion she didn't even have a name for.

She'd made that mistake three months ago and look what had happened.

Lia took a deep breath and moved over to the magnificent four-poster bed that stood against one wall. Opposite were windows that gave a view out over the mountains, the sharp, black shapes softened by the falling snow. Everything was white and silent.

The room itself was thickly carpeted in a dark charcoal, the walls a warm neutral white, nothing that would compete with the glory of the view. It might have felt cold if not for the rugs on the floor and the black fur thrown over the bed.

She paused beside the bed, looking down at the clothing that had also been thrown over it. A pair of cosy soft grey sweatpants and a dark blue hoodie. They looked huge.

Lia reached out and touched the fabric of the hoodie. It felt as soft as it looked.

These were his, weren't they?

*Lia stood at the window of her bedroom that overlooked the famous gardens of the palace. It was early, but she'd woken up and hadn't been able to get back to sleep.*

*She'd looked out to see what kind of day it was supposed to be since her mother had told her that she was having riding lessons today; Matias liked to ride apparently so she would have to learn. And she'd seen a dark figure running down one of the long paths.*

*It was cold, nearly winter, and the fig-ure wore long, dark sweat pants and a dark hoodie. He was jogging, not fast, but not slow, and she could tell already by the pres-*

*ence of the guards that kept pace with him that it was the Regent.*

*Her heart beat faster.*

*She hadn't met him yet—she hadn't been important enough for an introduction—but she would. Once her father brought up the subject of her prospective engagement to Matias, of course.*

*Meanwhile, ever since he'd arrived at the palace, she'd been fascinated with him. She'd read everything published on the web about him, all the gossip columns and business pages.*

*The Spanish Bastard, the media had dubbed him. A shark, they said. A financial genius who'd built a global, multi-billion-dollar company from the seed of one small finance company in Barcelona, in just a few short years. A dangerous man, cold and calculating, who now ran Santa Castelia as efficiently as one of his own companies.*

*People were wary of him and with good reason. He was ruthless. And he was everything the media said about him, at least according to her father. But he also had a strong moral code, which was why Gian had brought him to Santa Castelia to rule. He'd included Matias in his decision making, teaching him about the business of ruling, and she'd once personally watched as the child of one of the palace staff had mistakenly run into him one day out in the grounds. Everyone had held their breath, waiting to see what he'd do, since if he'd been Carlos he would have punished both the child and the parent. But all he'd done was pick the child up, checked to see if he was okay, then set him on his feet, and had gone on with the meeting he was in the middle of as if nothing had happened.*

*A hard man, they said, and he was. But he wasn't cruel. He wasn't his father and that, if nothing else, proved it.*

*Lia watched him jog around and around the perimeter of the gardens, fascinated by the fluid way he moved. Easy and loose, with a long, loping stride.*

*Then finally when he stopped, right by her window, he tugged the hoodie off and over his head, revealing the hard, muscular lines of his torso, clearly outlined by the T-shirt he wore underneath.*

*Every time she'd seen him, he'd been in one of his meticulously tailored dark suits, but now he was in sweatpants and a T-shirt that clung to every line, showing off the carved musculature of his wide shoulders and powerful chest, the dips and hollows of his abs.*

*Her breath caught.*

*He wasn't built like a businessman. He was built like a warrior.*

*She'd only just turned eighteen and was sheltered. Her life revolving around her schooling and the lessons in queenship that her parents had insisted on. Men—boys— had never factored into anything she did. And why would they? She was promised to only one man and that man was Matias.*

*Except Matias wasn't a man, not yet. He was a boy and it had never been so obvious until this moment. Where she realised that Matias had never made her breath catch the way it did just now. She'd never wanted to look at him the way she wanted to look at Rafael Navarro. Never wanted to see what his chest looked like underneath the fabric of his T-shirt, never wanted to touch...*

Lia shivered, memory tightening its grip. The first awakening of her sexuality and not for the man she should have wanted, but for a man so forbidden she shouldn't have been looking at him that way at all.

But she had.

She'd been naive, thinking that looking wasn't a crime. Not realising the power of her own obsession with him or understanding the feelings he'd awakened in her.

Her life was so curtailed, everything she did needing her parents' approval first. Her friendships were monitored, every activity needing to be signed off, and it had been dull. So dull. There had been no excitement in her life, nothing new.

He had been the first person she'd met who'd felt dangerous and exciting and she'd wanted more of him.

*And now you have more and you're baulking.*

Lia abruptly shrugged out of her wedding

gown, gathering the soft, heavy folds and laying it carefully on the bed. Then she picked up the sweatpants and hoodie and went over to another door near the bed that led into an en-suite bathroom.

Tiled in pristine white, the room felt open and airy, the floor warm beneath her icy feet. She stood in front of the mirror and discarded her veil, the diamond circlet and all the pins holding her hair in place. Her makeup had run, her eyes looking shadowed and black, her cheeks pale.

Her mother would be appalled to see her like this. She'd always hated Lia's wilder side, especially the adventures she'd had in the woods behind the palace gardens, climbing the trees and making forts, and playing illicit games of war with some of the other palace children.

Lia would come home with filthy, torn clothes and wild hair, and receive a lecture from her mother about how a future queen needed to be immaculate.

She was not immaculate now.

*What kind of thanks is that for all your parents' hard work?*

Something that felt like grief wound through her and she turned away from her reflection, forcing the thought from her head.

She didn't want to think about her parents, not yet.

Instead, she got rid of her underwear, then stepped under the shower, letting the stream of blissfully hot water warm her up and wash away the memories of the day.

As the water fell around her, she gently touched the slightly rounded curve of her stomach and a wave of protectiveness went through her. She had no idea what kind of mother she would be, but she certainly wasn't going to weigh her child down with a heavy load of expectations the way she had been.

She wasn't going to tell them how hard she had worked for them or how difficult it had been to conceive. How many tears had been shed and heartache endured simply for the privilege of having her.

She wouldn't lecture them about the sacrifices that had been made and how her happiness was dependent on theirs, and didn't they owe her that? Hadn't she been through enough for them?

*So much for not thinking about your parents.*

Her hand cupped her stomach as the grief turned into a sharp, painful kind of anger. Then from out of nowhere, Rafael's voice drifted through her head.

*'That was what they wanted, Lia. You said yourself that no one ever asked you what you wanted. They didn't even think about you... So why nail yourself to a cross you didn't even build?'*

She'd told herself for years that she was happy with the opportunities her parents had given her, because that's how they'd phrased the betrothal to Matias. An opportunity to prove her worth and make them proud, as her father had said. As if just existing wasn't enough and she had to do something more.

She hadn't questioned it. Her mother had talked a lot about how hard it had been to conceive and that by the time they'd gone through the IVF process, they were older parents. And that they didn't have the energy for a child as 'volatile and high maintenance' as she had been.

She loved her parents and so she'd tried to be good, to control the worst of her behaviours. To not have tantrums when she was angry or cry when she was upset, or shriek too loudly when she was having fun. To be well behaved and good, and to never give them a reason to regret having her.

She'd done that for years without question.

Until one night when she couldn't sleep, she'd been out walking the palace halls and had found the door to her father's office open. And she'd gone inside, because she was curious, poking around and finding a whisky bottle and a box of cigars.

Because it was midnight and no one was around, she'd taken a sip of that whisky. Then she'd tried one of those cigars. She'd felt reckless and rebellious, all the things she never allowed herself to feel during the day, and so she'd kept doing it.

Then one night Rafael had caught her. She'd brazened it out by offering him a glass of whisky, which he'd then shocked her by taking. Then he'd sat down and they'd talked and talked. She'd thought it had been a one-off, but a couple of days later he'd come back and they'd resumed talking.

She'd realised then that he didn't care about her behaviour. That she didn't have to moderate herself with him, that he *liked* her when she was 'volatile'.

Just as she'd liked him. And then more than liked. She'd *wanted*...

*And you still do, so why not have a night with him? Just one. And maybe it will vanquish this need for both of you.*

Lia blinked through the water running down over her face, the thought catching her unawares, making her stomach swoop and dive.

As she'd already thought, she had the luxury of choice now. While she didn't want to marry him, that didn't mean she couldn't sleep with him.

Three months ago she'd chosen to go to Matias and it had only been an accident that had led her to Rafael's bed. But she could choose differently now.

Now she had the freedom to choose him because she wanted him, not so she could forget him. And he was hungry for her, too. She'd loved that. Loved how desired he'd made her feel that night.

So why couldn't she have that again? Why couldn't they both have it?

Lia turned off the water and got out. She dried herself on a warm, fluffy white towel, then pulled her underwear back on and dressed in the sweats that had been on the bed.

They were clean, smelling of laundry powder, but there was no doubt as to whose they were, because they swamped her. The pants weren't so bad because she had a little baby bump, plus they had a drawstring she could pull tight around her hips, but the hoodie was a different story. It swamped her, extending down to her knees and she had to roll the sleeves up hugely.

She was wearing his clothes. His. *Rafael's.*

Lia took a deep breath.

Yes, she would. She and Rafael were cut off, alone. No court to watch them, no parliament to answer to, no media to track their every move. What happened here no one would ever know about. There was no one to judge her, no one at all.

She didn't know what her future was going to look like and that was terrifying, but tonight was certain and he was here.

A rush of something went through her, excitement, anticipation, or something else, she couldn't tell what, but she grabbed on to it with both hands and held on tight.

*What about marrying him? What about wanting to be chosen? What about giving in?*

Sex didn't have to mean marriage and she wasn't giving in. She was choosing for herself. And while he might not have wanted to marry her if she wasn't pregnant, he *did* want to sleep with her. He'd chosen her in that sense.

*And your heart? What about that?*

But Lia ignored that thought. Her heart had nothing to do with this. For the first time in her life she could do what *she* wanted to do, not what anyone else wanted her to do, and that's all that mattered.

Rafael kept tabs on the calls, social media notifications and emails that kept pouring in, while at the same time monitoring the state of the weather via the internet.

They'd be cut off from the outside world for some time since it was clear it wasn't going to stop snowing any time soon and all the mountain passes were blocked.

As he hadn't managed to get Lia's agreement on the marriage idea yet, he continued to maintain radio silence with the outside world. Which he wasn't sorry about in the slightest since it meant they would remain undisturbed.

Constanza delivered refreshments to the living room, small perfect sandwiches and delicate cut fruit. Some pastries as well as orange juice and a pot of coffee.

Rafael dismissed her and set out the food himself, arranging it just so on the coffee table in front of the fire.

The room was nicely warm now, the snow

outside making it seem as though it was dark, even though night was still a few hours away.

It felt cosy, intimate, reminding him of Gian's study all those months ago, the first time he'd walked in…

*Rafael paced along the echoing hallways of the palace. It was late and he couldn't sleep. He often couldn't, there was too much going on in his head, and so he roamed the palace at night, trying to solve the day's problems with some good old-fashioned pacing.*

*He'd been surprised to find out how much he enjoyed being Regent—it was just the kind of challenge he liked—and he'd enjoyed being a big brother, too. More than he'd anticipated. Matias had got over his wariness after the first couple of months and had thrown himself into the business of learning how to be King. He'd proved to be a quick study and had blossomed over the past couple of years. He would be a good king for Santa Castelia, Rafael was sure.*

*His footsteps rang on the old stone floor as he strode down one of the narrower hallways.*

*He'd dismissed his guards for the night and it was good to be alone, since he hardly ever was. It gave him time to think.*

*One of the doors in the hall stood slightly open, light shining through.*

*Afterwards, he was never sure what had made him stop since an open doorway wasn't unusual, though it was late for someone to have a light on. Perhaps it was the faint, aromatic scent of cigar smoke drifting into the hallway that made him stop. Because that scent was familiar. Gian smoked cigars that smelled like that.*

*He took a quick look around, orienting himself, and realised he must be standing outside Gian's office. It seemed the first advisor was still working, even though it was late.*

*Rafael went to the door and pushed it open, wondering what was keeping the old man up till nearly midnight. But it wasn't Gian who sat at his desk.*

*The desk lamp was on, casting a warm glow in the small room. Bookshelves lined the walls, the shelves crammed not only with*

*books but keepsakes, photos, bits of statio-
nery, letters and all kinds of other things.*

*The desk itself was oak, large and heavy,
the surface of the desktop scattered with pens
and paper, a computer screen and an old key-
board, a blotter that had been doodled on,
and old cups of coffee.*

*And a pair of pretty bare feet, complete
with blue toenails.*

*Rafael blinked.*

*A woman sat back in Gian's chair with her
feet on the desk. In one long-fingered hand
she held a crystal tumbler full of an amber
liquid that had to be alcohol of some kind
and in the other a lit cigar.*

*It was Amalia, Gian's daughter. The same
daughter who was promised to Matias.*

*Rafael had met her only once before, when
Gian had shown him the agreement between
Carlos and himself that Carlos's son would
marry her. A match that Rafael had no issue
with since the De Vita family was ancient aristocracy and very suitable.*

*He hadn't paid any particular attention to
her. She was pretty, answering all his ques-*

*tions in a low, nearly inaudible voice. She didn't meet his gaze and was so self-effacing he'd almost forgotten she was there. He had tried to make conversation with her, but had eventually given up when all the conversational balls he'd lobbed in her direction were not lobbed back.*

*Matias had told him she was dull and it turned out he was right.*

*Except the woman sitting with her feet on the desk, sipping what looked like whisky and smoking a cigar, was the very antithesis of dull.*

*Her black hair was loose, a glossy, inky waterfall over her shoulders, and all she wore was a white nightgown that would have been virginal if the fabric hadn't been so sheer he could see right through it. She was staring at him, her deep blue eyes gone very dark and very round, her luscious mouth in a perfect O of surprise. Her cheeks flooded with pink and for a second neither of them moved, both of them staring at each other in shock.*

*It hit him then, the sudden, hard kick of a desire he should never have felt.*

*But the feeling was so wrong that he crushed it before he'd even had the chance to feel it.*

*'What are you doing here?' he asked curtly.*

*Her mouth closed and something shifted in her eyes, though he couldn't tell what it was. Thick, silky sable lashes descended, veiling her gaze, and he thought she'd apologise, get to her feet, and move quietly out the door.*

*But she didn't.*

*'It's my father's study,' she said instead. 'I'm allowed to be here.'*

*He stilled. She sounded almost...challenging, which he hadn't expected.*

*Her lashes rose then, an irresistible glow in her eyes. 'Perhaps you'd like to join me for a drink, Your Excellency?'*

He should never have gone in. Never have sat down in the armchair opposite her. Never have allowed his curiosity to get the better of him, wanting to know why she was in her father's study, smoking cigars and drinking his whisky.

He should never have started that first conversation, that had led to all the others and eventually her in his bed as passion had exploded between them.

But he'd told himself it was only conversation, that he had to get to know his future sister-in-law, to make sure she really was as suitable for Matias as she appeared.

And she wasn't suitable for Matias, it turned out. Not suitable at all.

*But she's perfect for you.*

Rafael ignored that as a small figure appeared in the doorway, a small figure swamped by the far-too-big hoodie she wore.

Lia.

Her hair was damp and curling in waves down her back, the sleeves of the hoodie rolled up. She wore sweatpants and the hems of those, too, were rolled up nearly to her knees.

His clothes. But of course. He'd ordered Constanza to find her something to wear, yet he didn't have any women's clothes here. The only clothes available would be his.

The coiling possessiveness tightened once more, because he liked that. He liked that *very* much. It appealed to the territorial male inside him that the woman pregnant with his child was safe in his house, wearing his clothes. Protected by him.

His.

*Careful. She's not yours.*

No, but she would be. He'd decided. He'd make it happen.

She lifted her chin as their gazes met, as if daring him to comment.

He obliged. 'I see Constanza found you some clothing.'

'Yes. Yours, I assume?'

'Mine,' he agreed. 'It suits you.' And it did.

It wasn't that spectacular wedding gown, but somehow the oversized clothing drew attention to her femininity in a way that made him want to pick her up and hold her close.

'I'm not sure that's a compliment,' she said, then gave him a look that went through him like a quarrel from a crossbow, the same look she'd given him that night in her father's study. Her eyes had been so blue, glowing with a challenge he hadn't been able to resist...

'Perhaps you'd like to join me for a drink?' he murmured, in a very deliberate and conscious echo of her invitation that night.

Lia blinked, an expression he couldn't quite put his finger on flickering over her delicate features. Colour warmed her cheeks and then, like the sun coming out, she smiled.

His heart kicked hard inside his chest, his breath catching.

She'd been so generous with those smiles, making him feel as though he'd been given the most precious gift whenever she turned them on him. No one else smiled at him like that. No one else smiled at him at all.

He missed them.

'I'd love to,' she said, the warmth in her expression making him ache. 'But make it an orange juice.'

'And no cigars.' His voice sounded rough and he couldn't seem to smooth it over.

'What a pity.' Her smile faded, her gaze meeting his with a directness that took his breath away. 'I miss those nights with you.'

His heart jerked again, the ache inside him spreading out.

\* \* \*

'Prospective queens shouldn't be drinking whisky and smoking cigars,' he said, coming into the study and standing in front of Gian's desk.

'Perhaps someone should have told King Carlos that.' Her tone was dry, her blue eyes full of humour and something else, a very definite and most unexpected challenge.

'King Carlos was not a prospective queen,' he pointed out. 'He was a king.'

Amalia lifted her tumbler very pointedly and took a sip. 'Not a very good one.'

His interest, already caught, deepened. She was not at all the way she'd appeared to him the week before at their first meeting, with her gaze lowered and only speaking when she'd been spoken to.

How...interesting.

'Agreed.' Slowly, he sat down in the armchair before the desk and watched as she took her pretty feet off the desktop and began to rummage in one of the drawers. A second later, she'd pulled out another glass, pro-

*duced the bottle of very good Scotch and poured him a measure.*

*'Does your father know who's drinking his best whisky?' he asked as she pushed the tumbler across the desktop to him.*

*'No.' She gave him a direct look. 'And you're not going to tell him.'*

*'Am I not? No one gives orders to the Regent,* princesa.*'*

*She pulled a face. 'I'm not a princess.'*

*He lifted the tumbler and took a sip. It was indeed very good Scotch. 'Then give me one good reason why I shouldn't tell your father right now that I caught you in his office, stealing his good alcohol and smoking his cigars.'*

*She capped the whisky, leaned back in her chair, picked up her cigar again and took a drag. Then blew a perfect smoke ring. 'Because I'll be sad if you do?'*

*Dull, Matias had said. Yes, the woman sitting at the desk was not dull, not in the slightest. It surprised him and he was so seldom surprised.*

*'That is not a convincing argument,' he said mildly, amused despite himself.*

*She gave him the sweetest smile. 'Well, other rebellions aren't permitted so I have to take mine where I find them. Also, I can hardly advise Matias on the dangers of drinking and smoking if I haven't tried them myself, can I?'*

*Women had always fallen into two camps for Rafael. They were either associated with work, in which case they were off limits, or they were prospective sexual partners. It wasn't a conscious choice on his part, that was just how it had happened. Mainly due to the fact that he never had a shortage of women throwing themselves at him, either for his sexual prowess or for a taste of his power.*

*But he felt something unfamiliar twist inside him as he looked into Lia's blue eyes.*

*She didn't seem afraid of him and she wasn't seeking his approval, or jockeying for his attention. And she looked at him as if he was a person, not the Regent. Not the CEO of a multinational company and not a powerful man to seduce. Not the Spanish Bastard, the unwanted mistake of an unpopular king.*

*But him. Rafael.*

*And he knew the feeling was dangerous, that he should get up and walk away. Yet he didn't. He sat there and he looked back at her and said, 'No, this is true. What other rebellions have you tried?'*

'There is no need to miss them, *princesa,*' he murmured, the ache in his heart getting heavier at the memories. 'We can have them again, I promise.'

She lifted one black brow. 'But only if I marry you, yes?'

'*Sì.*'

Interestingly, this didn't seem to annoy her as much as it had earlier, because she only nodded before sitting herself regally on the couch. 'The promised orange juice, if you please.'

Despite the strange heaviness in his chest, amusement flickered through him. 'Do you expect me to wait on you, Lia?'

She gave him a cool look, every inch of her queenly. 'Yes.'

It made him smile. She was ridiculously appealing like this.

'Your wish. My command.' He moved over to the coffee table and poured her a glass of orange juice, then held it out to her. She took it and he made sure that their fingertips didn't brush.

Judging from that feeling in his chest, his control was suspect so it was best that he tried to limit temptation.

Lia took a sip of her orange juice, then leaned back on the couch, her blue eyes lifting to his. 'Why marriage? Why is that so very important to you?'

He frowned, the question unexpected. 'I told you. I don't want our son or daughter having to—'

'No,' she interrupted calmly. 'I don't think that's the reason. Or at least not the real reason.'

Rafael tensed, though he wasn't sure why. 'What makes you say that?'

'There aren't many men who'd throw a woman over their shoulder and carry her off from the church on the day of their wedding, before absolutely *insisting* on marrying her themselves.' She took another sip, her gaze on his very steady. 'That's a drastic course of action simply to spare your child a couple of derogatory names. Especially for men who don't like scandal.'

He didn't like talking about his mother, but there was no reason not to tell Lia. 'My mother was a single parent,' he said shortly. 'My father got her pregnant, then left her alone in Barcelona with no means of support. It was a miserable existence for her and it left her very unhappy, and I will not do the same.'

'But there is financial support. You don't need—'

'Marriage also gives a degree of legal protection both to you and the child.' He still felt tense. 'I know you want to be chosen, Lia. In which case you should know that I have never proposed marriage to anyone before. You are the first and the only.'

She lifted a shoulder. 'Yes, but as I pointed out to you earlier, only because I'm pregnant. It would never have entered your head if I wasn't.'

Frustration wound through him. He didn't

know what more she wanted from him. 'You were Matias's bride. Of course it never entered my head.'

'And if I hadn't been?'

He shoved his hands into his pockets. 'What exactly are you asking me, Lia?'

She looked back for a long moment, then abruptly put down her juice. Her blue gaze was suddenly very, very direct. 'If I hadn't been Matias's bride, would you have married me, Rafael?'

# CHAPTER SIX

IT WAS A dangerous question to ask and she knew it. But she couldn't help herself.

Rafael stood on the other side of the coffee table, the fire leaping behind him and outlining his tall, masculine figure. He'd discarded his jacket and waistcoat, wearing only the tastefully striped trousers in light and dark grey and a simple white shirt. It suited him, highlighting his olive skin and black hair, the clean lines of his broad shoulders and lean waist.

He stood casually, apparently relaxed with his hands in his pockets. Yet his silver eyes burned.

She'd come downstairs, intending to greet any more seduction attempts with a definitive yes, only to have him organise food, pour her orange juice, then try to push his marriage agenda on her, which was not what she wanted.

But then he'd reminded her of those nights together, of how they'd talked and discussed and argued. And a sudden realisation had gripped her—that though she might know how his brilliant mind worked, how science interested him and what he thought about the latest political situation in Europe, she had no idea about anything else.

There were facts about his life that she knew from her internet research, but that's all they were. Just facts. And while she did know now what made him growl in the dark and what made him groan with pleasure, she'd didn't know his heart. She didn't know his hopes or his dreams or what he'd wanted to be when he grew up.

None of that should have mattered to her, not when she wasn't going to be marrying him no matter what he thought, so she wasn't sure why it felt so imperative now.

Yet the curiosity that gripped her felt more important than anything else. More important even than sex.

'No,' he said, his stare unwavering. 'I wouldn't have married you.'

A small, sharp pain shot through her. She ignored it.

'Why not?'

'Because a wife wasn't something I ever wanted.'

'So, what did you want then?'

His expression didn't change. 'To rule Santa Castelia to the best of my ability. Fill its treasury. Make sure the heir will be a decent king when he comes of age.'

'And then what?'

'What do you mean?'

'What did you want after that? Presumably, since you didn't want a wife or children, you had other plans. So, what were they?'

Something in his eyes flickered. 'It doesn't matter what they were. Nothing changes the situation we have to deal with now.'

'It does matter,' she disagreed. 'No one ever asked me what I wanted, Rafael, and I wonder if anyone had ever asked you the same. So now I'm asking. What do *you* want?'

A muscle flicked in his jaw. He was tense

and she didn't know why. It was clear something about her question bothered him.

'You,' he said roughly. 'I want you in my bed.'

A pulse of an answering heat went through her, but she pushed it aside. This was important. They'd never had the opportunity to talk about any of this and now they did. While she still hadn't changed her mind about marrying him, she wanted at least to understand him.

'That's not what I'm asking,' she said steadily. 'Did you want happiness? Success and a long life? More money? More power? Another country to rule?'

He was silent, the silver of his eyes blazing like liquid mercury. 'Why do you want to know these things? What purpose could knowing them possibly serve?'

'Isn't it obvious? I want to know you.'

That muscle flicked in his jaw again, his tall figure radiating tension. 'You know me already, Lia.'

'No, I don't. I know that you like whisky and Cuban cigars. And I know your thoughts on various political situations. I know you don't like the word "no".' She swallowed, a familiar, relentless ache unwinding inside her. The ache to get closer to him, to scratch the surface of him and find out what lay beneath. 'But those are all just parts of you. I don't know the whole. I know the Regent and bits and pieces of the man, but I want the rest, Rafael. If you want me to marry you, I *have* to know.'

Again, he stayed silent, merely staring at her.

'How long?' he demanded suddenly. 'How long have you wanted me?'

She didn't want to tell him because of what it would reveal, but then again, why not? Why shouldn't he know? She could hardly demand answers from him and then not give them herself.

'Ever since you arrived at the palace,' she said baldly.

'But you were only—'

'Seventeen, yes. Maybe I didn't quite know what it meant at the time, but over the years I worked it out, believe me.'

His gaze flared, though nothing else about him moved.

But she'd had months of those meetings in her father's study, of looking into his eyes, watching his face. Watching him.

She'd shocked him, hadn't she?

'Lia,' he said finally.

'What? I know you didn't feel the same way then, don't worry.'

Another long moment passed and then abruptly he turned and moved over to the fire, his back to her.

He was so tall, so broad. Outlined in flames he seemed somehow otherworldly. A demon or a dark angel, or even the Devil himself come to take her soul.

An eon passed and then he said, his voice roughened, 'Why? Why did you feel that way about me? I didn't even know you existed.'

She leaned forward and picked up her orange juice again, sipping at it, staring at his dark figure. He'd changed the subject, directing the topic away from himself, and now he'd turned away from her. Why? What was he trying to hide? Or did he not want to see her face?

Perhaps he needed honesty from her first before he shared anything with her and that was okay. She understood. Someone had to make the first move and it was clear that it wasn't going to be him. And there was probably a reason for that.

A thread of stubborn determination wound through her, tightening.

She'd hated all the expectations heaped on her—yes, she could admit that now—yet she'd done the same thing to him. Thinking she knew him when, really, she didn't.

She had to stop. She had to discover the man he actually was, not the man she'd always thought he was, and to do that she was going to have to give him the same honesty she demanded of him, earn his trust.

*Why? When you've decided you're not marrying him?*

Well, all those nights they'd spent talking together had formed a bond of friendship surely? So that made him her friend. And friends trusted each other.

*It's not friendship you feel for him.*

Her heartbeat speeded up, her breath catching, a knowledge she'd been avoiding shifting inside her, making her feel strangely vulnerable and uncertain.

He couldn't be more than a friend to her, that had never been allowed. Besides, hadn't she decided her feelings were of the teenage crush variety?

*It is allowed now.*

But something cold wound through and she shoved the thought away.

'I watched you arrive at the palace,' she said into the silence. 'I saw you get out of the limo. Everyone around me was scared of you, but the moment I saw you I knew there was nothing to be afraid of. You were strong and powerful, but…steady. Calm. In control. I knew you weren't going to be like Carlos. You were going to be different.'

He gave a rough laugh that held nothing but bitterness. '*Si.* So different that I got my brother's fiancée pregnant.'

So, he blamed himself. He thought that night together was his fault. His mistake and now, here he was, taking responsibility. Fixing it.

To hell with that.

'I wasn't his fiancée at the time,' she said. 'That didn't happen until after.'

'You were his intended. You've been intended for him since you were both three years old.'

'It wasn't just you in that bed, Rafael. It was me as well.'

'You were young. You were an innocent. You had no idea—'

'What I was doing?' Lia pushed herself to her feet, possessed by a sudden and intense need to take this burden from him or at least to share it.

He was always taking responsibility for things, always fixing things, and she understood that was his role, but he wasn't the Regent with her.

With her, he'd always been just Rafael.

'Yes, I was virgin and I let my feelings get the better of me,' she went on. 'I let my anger take control. But I could have got out of that bed at any time and I didn't.'

'You were inexperienced,' he said, ignoring her. 'Passion like that is so rare and once it takes hold of you—'

'Rafael, will you stop talking and listen to me!'

He turned from the fire suddenly and this time the expression on his face matched the fury in his eyes.

'I won't be thought of as a man who engages in casual affairs, sowing his seed far and wide,' he said harshly. 'I won't be a man who can't control himself. You will marry me and we'll tell the press some story of how it was some grand passion we both couldn't deny. That will reduce the scandal surrounding the throne at least and make Matias look less weak. And a marriage will be proof that it wasn't just a casual affair.'

She swallowed as a small shard of pain caught inside her, surprising her. Did he really think that? Because that night he'd been a force of nature, his unleashed passion sweeping her away. She'd hoped to forget Rafael in Matias's arms, but the opposite had happened.

She'd forgotten Matias instead and not only him, but her position as princess. She'd forgotten her parents and the weight of all those expectations.

She'd forgotten her country.

She'd forgotten her own name.

That night she'd been just a woman in the arms of a man she wanted and there had been nothing but the excitement of discovery and heat, and the heady blaze of a pleasure burned into her memory for ever.

The last thing it had ever been was casual.

'Is that how you view it, Rafael?' she asked, trying not to sound as if it mattered so very much when the opposite was true. 'Do you think that night we shared was just a casual affair?'

He said nothing, his expression closing down all of a sudden, as if all that fury had been doused.

And the feelings inside her tangled abruptly together in a tight, hard ball. Anger and pain and confusion, and a bright, hot need that surely felt too strong to be a mere teenage crush.

'It was never casual to me,' she said starkly, giving him the truth, unable to hold it back. *'Never.'*

He was very, very still. Every line of him radiated tension, as if there was something violent inside him struggling to get out and he couldn't let go of the leash, not for an instant.

'You want to know what it meant to me? You really want to know?' Those silver eyes of his blazed. 'Come here and I'll show you.'

Lia didn't hesitate, didn't second-guess. She'd already decided in the bedroom upstairs what she wanted and so she moved around the coffee table, coming closer. And he didn't look away, as if he couldn't take his eyes off her. And she was back again at that ball three months earlier...

*The palace gardens had been lit beautifully for the gala, one of Santa Castelia's most anticipated social events, the last celebration of summer. It was always held outside and the weather had turned out perfectly, the intense heat of the day fading into a lovely soft warmth. Lights were strung in all the trees, more lights were wrapped around shrubs and statues and trellises. Fountains played and music drifted in the air. Palace staff moved among the crowd, carrying trays of drinks and food.*

*All of Santa Castelia's aristocracy were there, along with the nation's rich and famous. There were also more than a few international stars and captains of industry, because the late summer gala had a reputation for being a good party.*

*Lia stood next to Matias by one of the fountains, half listening to him talk with her father and a few government officials, half watching the crowds swirl around them.*

*Some of the women wore the most incredibly beautiful gowns, off the shoulder, plunging necklines, or some with a split up the thigh. Some glittered with sequins, while others looked like liquid satin, hugging every curve.*

*She envied the women who could wear gowns like that. She wasn't permitted anything that would show too much skin or be risqué, and her mother had advised her not to wear bold colours, that neutrals were more... decorous.*

*She hadn't been all that happy with Lia's choice of colour tonight—a bias-cut gown of deep, violet silk that gave a hint of her curves, but nothing too showy—but she'd let Lia wear it after she'd pleaded.*

*Just once she'd wanted to wear something that she felt pretty in, that didn't make her feel as if she was fading into the background, even though that was what was required of her, all the better to show off her future husband.*

*Matias hadn't commented on her gown and that was fine, it wasn't him she was wearing it for.*

*The crowd swirled and she watched, looking for a familiar, tall, broad figure, desperate to spot him. He hadn't joined her in her father's study for an entire week now and she wanted to know why. He hadn't told her anything. Just one night he hadn't turned up. She'd told herself it was a one-off, nothing serious, but then he hadn't come the next night either, or the one after that.*

*She wasn't able to talk to him, though she'd tried to surreptitiously ask for an audience since it was next to impossible trying to get time alone with him. Yet all her requests had been refused. She was starting to think that he was avoiding her and she didn't understand why.*

*Had she said something he hadn't liked? Done something, maybe? At their last meeting, their conversation had strayed into the personal a little, but surely that wouldn't have made him stop coming? Maybe she'd offended him...*

*Her heartbeat thudded and her palms felt sweaty. She wanted to move, to walk around and see if she could spot him, because standing here suddenly felt impossible.*

*Murmuring an excuse to Matias, she moved through the crowds, trying to look as though she was going somewhere, when in fact she was searching. Searching for him.*

*Then just when she thought that maybe he wasn't here, she caught a glimpse of his tall figure. He was standing in one of the arbours, surrounded by people, since he inev-*

*itably was always surrounded by people. A woman was talking to him, a beautiful blonde in a red gown with a plunging neckline and he was looking at her with that silver-eyed intensity that always made Lia's breath catch.*

*It did now, though not in that way that sent a rush of dizzying pleasure through her when they were alone. This time it felt like a stab through the chest.*

*He wore formal evening clothes, all in black, even his shirt, and with his massive height and warrior's build, his innate authority, he was the most intensely charismatic man in the entire place.*

*Except she knew things about him that other people didn't. Such as what he looked like when midnight struck and he was relaxed and nursing a tumbler of Scotch. When he was leaning back in his chair, no jacket or tie, the top buttons of his shirt undone and his sleeves rolled up. When their conversation was idle, on subjects that weren't of any importance, such as the thriller he was reading. Or the latest scientific advance he'd heard about, since he liked science, particu-*

*larly technology, and liked to keep abreast of what was happening.*

*When she made some silly joke and he smiled.*

*No one knew him when he was like that. No one knew him when he smiled.*

*No one but her.*

*She tried to tell herself that she had something of him the woman he was talking to didn't, hoping it would make her feel better. That she wasn't feeling jealous, not at all. She shouldn't be jealous anyway, because there was nothing to be jealous about. She was going to marry Matias and the Regent wasn't for her. He was older than she was, more experienced, more powerful, more...everything.*

*It didn't matter that the blonde was flirting with him.*

*He wasn't Lia's and he never would be.*

*She was just about to turn around and find her way back to Matias, when unexpectedly Rafael glanced at her over the woman's shoulder.*

*And his silver eyes met hers. And held.*

*And she knew that she'd let slip something*

she shouldn't and he'd seen what must have been in her gaze. Her whole soul.

He didn't look away, just stared at her.

Lia had no experience with men, none at all except for her interactions with Matias, which were friendly, but nothing more. She knew what sexual hunger and passion were, of course, but only intellectually.

Now though, she could feel both welling up inside her, a hot tide that felt as though it was choking her, a mirror of the same thing glowing in his eyes.

He felt it, too.

For a second they stared at each other, though it felt like hours, days. Eons. Then, without any hurry, he turned his gaze back to the woman in front of him and carried on talking to her as if nothing had happened.

Lia's face felt hot and tears pricked her eyes. Her chest was tight and painful and she didn't even know why.

It wasn't as though he could suddenly stop talking to that woman and come over to talk to her, not when everyone was watching him.

*Not when she was a woman he was barely supposed to even know, let alone speak to.*

*Their friendship—what else could she call it?—was secret and had to remain so.*

*Left with nothing else to do, Lia swallowed the ache inside her, buried it deep and turned and went back to Matias.*

But she didn't have to swallow that ache and she didn't have to turn away. Matias wasn't here and there was nothing between Rafael and her any longer.

So, she stood in front of him and looked into his burning gaze. 'Show me, then,' she said.

She was so close, looking at him the way she used to on those nights where they would argue about some philosophical topic or politics. Direct, fearless, challenging. They weren't talking about politics or philosophy, not now, yet the glow in her eyes was the same, a deep, aching blue with heat glowing at the centre, like fire in the dark heart of a sapphire.

But he was angry, he could feel it eating away at him, eating away at his control.

Angry at her for wanting him, for telling him that night had meant something to her when it would be so much easier for them both if it hadn't.

Angry at the questions she kept throwing at him, picking away at him, trying to get under his skin.

*'But those are all just parts of you. I don't know the whole...'*

She couldn't know the whole, that was the problem. Parts of him were all he had to give. The parts he had control over, not the ones he didn't.

The violent, hot, primitive parts of himself that no one needed to even know about, let alone see.

He'd managed to derail her by turning her questions back on her, yet that had rebounded on him to a certain extent. He'd had no idea how long she'd wanted him, or that she'd felt so passionately about their night together.

*You don't know her as well as you thought, do you?*

Perhaps he didn't. Perhaps he was just as guilty as everyone else, treating her just like the innocent, pure Crown Princess rather than the sharp, intelligent, fiery woman she actually was. And she *was* a woman, not a girl. A woman with her own needs and desires, as passionate and intense as he was…

He was supposed to be in control of himself. He wasn't supposed to let his hunger off the chain, because that was dangerous.

He was dangerous.

But…she wanted to know him. She wanted to know what that night had meant to him, so maybe it was time to show her. Let her see the parts of himself that he kept hidden. Not everything, of course, because no one needed to see those. Just the ones that could be shared in the dark.

So, he reached for her, his hands lifting, his fingers sliding through the black silk of her hair. Drawing her close so very slowly, because he had to be slow. He had to be careful otherwise the sheer weight of his hunger would crush them both.

She was breathing fast, too, looking at him

as though he was the only thing in her entire world. Her hands lifted to his chest, her palms pressing lightly against him, sending bolts of white lightning through him.

The sweetness of her scent surrounded him, making him feel hungry and lost and desperate.

*Careful. Be careful.*

Oh, he would. He'd let himself off the leash, but only a little. Just enough for her to get a taste, but no more.

'Lia,' he breathed. '*Princesa...mi princesa...*'

Her hands slid up his chest and around his neck and she was coming up on her toes, her mouth finding his.

And he was lost.

His fingers closed into fists in her hair and he was kissing her hard and deep, as if the existence of the entire world depended on this kiss and that it would end if he stopped.

So he didn't stop, he pushed his tongue into her mouth, tasting her, desperate for the flavour he remembered from that night, a sweetness he couldn't place though he'd spent all night searching for it. Honey or brown sugar or cinnamon, or some kind of heady combination of all three. She was delicious, every kind of good thing he'd ever tasted, and he couldn't get enough.

She gave a soft moan, her body going pliant against his, her arms tightening around his neck. Her mouth was hungry on his, the sharp edge of her teeth against his lips.

Electricity shot through him.

The night they'd spent together she'd been an innocent, all sweetly hesitant and uncertain. And despite the need in him, he'd had to go carefully with her.

But there was nothing hesitant or uncertain about her now. She was as starved as he was and just as demanding, and it was obvious that careful wasn't what she wanted.

Something in him snapped as her hands clawed open the buttons of his shirt and he broke the kiss, dragging that wretched hoodie up and over her head. Then he shoved down the sweatpants, too, dragged her down on to the soft silken rug in front of the fire and got her beneath him.

Her black hair spilled over the jewel-bright

colours of the rug, her cheeks flushed, her eyes black with desire as they looked up into his.

'Please, Rafael,' she whispered, reaching for him. 'Oh, please.'

She was pleading for him the way she had that night, holding nothing back, yet this time he could see it, her desire laid bare in her eyes.

It drove his own hunger to a sharp, bright point.

He had to be careful, so careful.

His hands shook as he pulled open his trousers before reaching down between her pale thighs, shoving aside the pretty lace of her knickers. Then, sliding his hands beneath the soft rounded curve of her bottom, he lifted her, positioning himself, before thrusting hard and deep, a groan escaping him as the intoxicating, slick heat of her sex gripped him tight.

She cried out, too, arching beneath him, her luscious mouth opening, red and swollen from his kiss. Her gaze was on his as he paused inside her, looking down at her, remembering that night, that moment when they were joined for the first time.

The memory swelled between them, filling the space, aching and hot and desperate.

Her face had been in darkness then, but he could see it now, lit by the fire, her skin rose and gold, flames reflected in her eyes. She looked at him as if he mattered, as if he was everything to her, and when she lifted her hand and touched his cheek, he felt something shift and turn inside him.

It was a feeling he couldn't name that pressed against his heart and it was familiar. He'd felt it then, too.

*Careful, remember? You hurt people.*

He remembered. But he wouldn't hurt her. He would *never* hurt her.

He reached for her hand, brought her fingers to his mouth and kissed the tips of them. Then the urge to move became too intense to ignore and he slid himself out, then back in again, a long, luxurious glide that made them both gasp.

Her hands touched him again, his face, his neck, his throat. Down through the halves of his open shirt to his chest. Touching him as if she couldn't get enough, as if she was starved for the feel of his skin.

He'd gone too long without a woman who wanted him like this.

He'd gone too long without *her.*

Three months of fighting it, of ignoring it. Of pretending the desire for her wasn't burning as hotly and as strongly as it had those nights in her father's study. Pretending that it hadn't grown, fed by that one long, hot night she'd been in his bed.

He'd pushed it aside, ignored it. Done the right thing and acted as though it hadn't happened. But it had. He'd ached, he'd burned and now that he had her here beneath him, he knew he couldn't let her go.

That baby was his, but so was she.

He slid his hands beneath her, gathering her close, pushing deeper, harder, driving them on because this couldn't last. The pleasure was much too strong.

She twisted in his arms, as if she was desperate to get closer, so he found her mouth and took it. Kissing her hard so that they were joined here, too.

Her arms wound around his neck and she moved with him, the pleasure becoming so acute it was almost painful.

The orgasm built and built, then it was flooding through him, drowning him in pleasure, and he could feel it take her, too, her body convulsing around his, a cry of release vibrating in her throat.

For long moments he lay there with her in his arms, unable to move. Unable to even think as aftershock after aftershock pulsed through him. Her face was turned into his neck and he could feel her warm breath against his skin, hear the ragged sound of it in his ear.

That intense possessiveness moved through him and he responded without thought, lifting his head and looking down at her sprawled out on the rug beneath him.

She was all pale silken skin, naked and perfect, the curve of her stomach where their child lay making everything in him want to growl.

'You are mine, Lia,' he said roughly, forcefully. 'You will marry me.'

She didn't move, looking up at him. Deep in the shadowed blue of her eyes, passion still smouldered. 'Okay,' she said.

Surprise rippled through him. He'd expected another refusal. 'What do you mean, okay?'

She lifted her hand, one delicate finger stroking his cheekbone in a featherlight touch. 'I mean, yes, I will marry you.'

# CHAPTER SEVEN

LIA HAD MADE the decision as she lay beneath him, staring up into his eyes and seeing his desperation and desire, all the blazing intensity that he hid from other people, but never from her.

He needed her, she understood, though what it was that he needed she didn't know. He probably didn't even realise it himself, but that didn't change the fact that he did.

Lots of people had expected things from her, but no one had ever *needed* her. Not the way she sensed Rafael did. And he didn't require her to be anything or to act a certain way. All he'd wanted was for her to say yes to his proposal and be his wife.

That need had made something inside her echo in response, the ache that she'd never been able to ignore or force away, that had lived in her heart growing deeper and stronger every time she saw him.

How could she let him bear sole responsibility for this and then deny him the means to fix it? If she said no, it would make everything harder and not only for herself and her child, but for him as well.

He was a bastard and he didn't want that for his child. What he wanted was to help her and, after what he'd said about his mother being a single parent, she could understand his motivation.

Denying him just because she wanted to be chosen for herself felt selfish, especially when all he was thinking of was what was best for their child.

So she wouldn't be selfish. And she wouldn't let him have to deal with this on his own.

She would marry him—after all, it wasn't exactly a life sentence. There would be considerable compensations.

His blazing stare narrowed. 'What? Just like that?'

'Yes.' She smiled at his suspicious expression. 'Just like that.'

He searched her face, though what he was looking for she had no idea. 'Why?' he demanded.

'Why?' Her finger brushed over his cheekbone again, loving the feel of his skin against hers. 'Because you're right, I have to think of our child and what's best for them, and I think being your wife will make things easier for all of us in the long run, especially when it comes to the press. And because I can't leave you to take sole responsibility for what happened.' She met his gaze squarely. 'I know I said I wanted to be chosen for myself, but that's making it all about me and I can't do that. Not when you'll suffer repercussions, too.'

The look in his eyes was full of something ferocious that she didn't understand, but it made her breath catch.

'Are you sure?' he asked roughly.

Lia stroked her finger across his cheekbone again, relishing the feel of him. Already she could feel that terrible, nagging ache inside her quieting, settling.

It was the right decision. She knew it in her bones.

'Yes,' she said. 'I'm sure.'

He said nothing, still staring at her intently, but she was starting to get distracted by the burnished bronze of his olive skin glowing in the firelight between the open halves of his shift and by the pulse at the base of his throat, the scattering of crisp black hair across his chest.

Oh, she wanted to see more. She wanted to see all of him. This wasn't enough to do him justice.

His body was pressing against hers, the weight of him reminding her of the intensity of the pleasure they'd just shared. She could feel the pulse of it still echoing inside her, could still feel *him* inside her.

Then suddenly Rafael bent and his mouth covered hers in a possessive, intense kiss, and there was nothing she could do but answer it. Kissing him back, desperate all at once to taste him, to drown their mutual hunger in passion.

There was nothing more to talk about now

anyway. She'd agreed to be his wife and she was happy with her decision. Especially if would meant getting more of him, just like this.

She pushed at his chest so that they rolled over again, him on his back, her on top.

The flames from the fire were hot, illuminating his face. The ice had disappeared, there was nothing but that liquid mercury left and it swallowed her whole.

Fierce desire and a blazing satisfaction flooded through her, because finally he was hers. A man so full of intensity and heat that his soul must be a bonfire and he was, truly, all hers.

She hadn't realised how badly she'd wanted that until now.

Lia kissed him hungrily and then rained a trail of hot kisses over his hard jaw and the strong arch of his neck. She pressed her mouth against the beating pulse at the base of his throat, tasting the salty, musky flavour of his skin.

He didn't stop her, letting her follow the trail down over his chest and further, tracing the lines of his abs to the open zip of his trousers. She pushed her hand down inside and found him, smooth and hot and hard, pressing against her palm. She squeezed him and he made a harsh, masculine growling sound that excited her.

She had no experience of any of this, but that didn't bother her. She wanted to explore him, look at him in the firelight, discover all the power contained in his hard, muscular body. Unleash the passion she knew burned beneath his icy, controlled surface.

She didn't have to hold back any more and neither did he.

Trailing her lips further down over the hard lines of his abs, she went lower, gripping him, licking the hard length of his sex, then taking him into her mouth.

He growled again, his hips arching, and then he said her name in a hoarse, desperate voice.

It thrilled her, made her feel powerful. For so long she'd been nothing but a vessel for her parents' dreams. For Matias's vision of a perfect queen. For the expectations of an entire nation.

She was never herself, never had any power of her own.

But she did now. Here before the fire with Rafael beneath her, she was strong. She could make the infamously hard, cool Prince Regent of Santa Castelia lose his mind.

So, she did, giving him as much pleasure as she could with her mouth, her teeth and her tongue, relishing the rich, exotic flavour of him. Until he pulled her away with desperate hands, tugging her on top of him, guiding her until she was sitting astride his hips.

He was still half dressed, his shirt open, his skin like warm satin against hers, and he was magnificent. A god. She ran her fingers across the hard expanse of his chest, unable to get enough of him, but he cursed roughly in Spanish under his breath and abruptly sat up.

His mouth closed on hers, his hands on her hips, lifting her up and then bringing her down on him, impaling her.

Pleasure was like a lightning strike, bolting up her spine, expanding like a blast wave, tearing a gasp from her. His arms closed around her, holding her tight as he began to move.

He was everywhere, surrounding her with his heat and his strength and the warm scent that was intrinsically Rafael. The taste of him was in her mouth, the hard demand of his lips on hers, and she was lost to everything, the outside world falling away.

The man holding her wasn't the Regent, forbidden to her and as unreachable as the stars. He was just Rafael. The man she'd talked with and argued with, and laughed with at night in her father's study, over whisky and cigars.

The man who would be her husband.

Lia closed her eyes and gave herself up to him, letting him take her away from the outside world, surrounding her in heat and pleasure, and the promise of more to come.

Rafael held Lia in his arms for long moments, her warm body relaxed against his. She'd turned her face against his chest, her breath ghosting over his skin. It seemed as if she'd fallen asleep, which she probably needed after what had happened earlier in the day.

He should feel good, holding her like this, but he didn't. Something felt wrong, his chest was tight, as if he couldn't get enough air.

Trying to go carefully so he didn't wake her, he shifted her from his chest and on to the rug. Grabbing the throw from the couch, he wrapped it around her and put a cushion underneath her head. She made a sweet little sound, curling into the throw and snuggling against the cushion.

The constriction in his chest became acute, the need to move holding him tight in his grip, and he stepped out into the hallway, striding to the stairs and going up them with no thought to where he was going.

A couple of minutes later, he found himself in his office, a warm, comfortable room down at the back of the second floor. It had windows that showcased Santa Castelia's magnificent mountains and the green forest that carpeted the slopes. Everything was outlined in white and black, the lowering sky making the view seem oddly oppressive.

Or maybe that was just his mood.

The need for air hadn't lifted, his chest ached and he rubbed at it absently as he crossed over to the heavy, oak desk that dominated the room.

Now she'd agreed to marry him, there were things he had to do, things to organise, a nation to face and a brother to talk to.

And he didn't want to do any of them. He wanted to hold Lia in his arms, touch the soft roundness of her stomach, where his child lay.

*She is doing this for you.*

The iron band around his chest tightened still further and he found himself looking at the doorway, as if he could still see her lying fast asleep by the fire, curled around the baby she carried.

She had clung to him as he'd touched her, as he'd taken her, driven mad by the way she'd taken him in her mouth, tasted him. So innocent and yet full of passion, inexperienced and yet desperate.

The combination had been too much for him, he hadn't been able to bear it. He'd wanted to get as close to her as he possibly could, so he'd hauled her away from him and into his arms, holding her tight against his chest, kissing her deeply as he'd thrust inside her. And felt her welcome him...

Her arms had closed around him and he'd felt her relax, felt her give herself up to him...

*Dios,* he didn't understand it. He'd ruined her, taken her future away from her and yet she'd told him she couldn't let him take sole responsibility for fixing this, that she didn't want him suffering from repercussions, too, and had agreed to marry him. Then she'd held him as if she never wanted to let him go.

Why? When he'd done nothing for her but give her pain?

*But isn't that what you always give people? Pain?*

His jaw tightened and he turned back to the window, crossing to it and putting his hands on the glass. The surface was cool, but not cool enough. It felt as if he was suddenly burning up inside, as if there was a volcano inside him, heat building and building and if he wasn't careful he would explode.

That was dangerous, so dangerous. He had to cool himself down somehow.

There was a door that led to an outside terrace, so he pulled it open and stepped outside.

Snow fell on his burning skin, stinging like acid, the cold so intense it stole his breath. He ignored it, striding to the parapet that bound the stone terrace and then back again, working out this burning feeling inside him with movement.

Why the hell was he feeling like this anyway? The sex had been great and she'd agreed to his proposal. They would be married as soon as he could arrange it and, once all the media furore had died down, everything would be fine. They could then get on to thinking about their future together.

*She's doing this for you and that's the problem.*

Rafael took in a deep breath, the cold scouring the inside of his lungs.

He didn't want to think about that, but he couldn't help himself. If she was doing this for him, then it meant she cared about him.

And he didn't like that thought, not one bit. Because why would she?

No one had ever cared about him all that much, not even his mother. And he sure as hell never had any kind of caring from his father, not that he'd wanted it anyway and definitely not from that old bastard.

Rafael put his hands on the stone of the parapet, ignoring the bite of ice against his palms, and leaned against it, trying to deal with the unease that gripped him.

Perhaps she didn't care that much about him. Perhaps she only thought she did. She was, after all, young and inexperienced, and their physical chemistry was intense. Maybe she'd mistaken passion for caring.

Anyway, it could have been worse. She could be in love with him and that was something he could never accept. Not when love was so destructive and caused so much pain.

*After all, what is there to love about you?*

He crushed that thought. This wasn't about him, this was about Lia. This was about making sure that whatever she felt for him didn't become something more. Luckily, he had a solution.

Whatever she felt for him, he'd simply ignore it and then it would die.

*What about if she gets bitter like your mother did?*

Then he wouldn't give her cause for bitterness. He'd pay attention to her, take care of her, he'd make her happy.

*Can you, though? Can you make anyone happy?*

The ice in the air around him had somehow crawled into his veins and had begun to wind through him.

He ignored it. Of course he'd make her happy. He'd give her everything she could ever need. A beautiful home and a child. Support for whatever career she wanted to take on. Company when she needed someone to talk to. Great sex to keep her satisfied.

He'd be an exemplary husband since wasn't that what husbands did?

Rafael took a breath and shoved himself away from the icy parapet, conscious that no matter what he'd just told himself, the cold hadn't touched the strange heat inside him. It kept building, kept burning.

Perhaps if he did some work, that would help. That would keep him on track and stop his mind from going on this endless track, this second-guessing himself when he never, *ever* second-guessed himself.

He turned back to the door, only to see it opening and a small figure standing in the doorway. She was wrapped up in that throw, her black hair spilling over her shoulders, her skin pale and bare and so very unprotected.

More heat flooded through him, along with an unfamiliar protectiveness.

'Rafael?' Lia wiped snow from her eyes. 'Are you okay? What are you doing out here?'

Instantly he was moving, striding through the falling snow to where she stood. 'Go inside,' he ordered. 'You'll catch your death.'

'But, what about—?'

'Inside.' He put his hands on her hips and gave her a gentle push so that she took a few steps back into the warmth of his office, then followed her in, closing the door.

She frowned, one hand clutching the throw

around her, the other reaching to brush the snow from his shoulders. Then she went up on her tiptoes and brushed it out of his hair, too.

'Me?' she murmured as she did so. 'What about you? And what were you doing out on the terrace in the middle of a blizzard, idiot man?'

Something in her tone gripped him and held him tight. She sounded as if she was already his wife and had been for years, a warm tenderness in the words that he didn't know what to do with.

It made him feel off balance and he was *never* off balance.

He was always the one in charge, the one who made the decisions. He was the CEO, the Prince Regent. He was never in doubt, yet today this small woman had turned everything he thought about himself on its head.

Rafael took her wrist in a firm but gentle grip and pulled her hand away from him. 'I needed some air. What are you doing here? I thought you were asleep.'

'I was, but I woke up and you weren't there.'

She didn't pull out of his hold, merely standing there and looking up at him. 'Are you all right?'

'Of course. Why would I not be?'

The crease between her fine, silky black brows deepened. 'You looked upset.'

He didn't like that she'd seen the doubt inside him, the uncertainty that no matter how much he told himself he didn't feel, he did all the same.

'I am not upset.' He kept his tone casual, betraying nothing. 'Perhaps you would like a shower or a bath? You have some time. Dinner will be in a few hours.'

She was quiet a moment, just looking at him. 'You don't like talking about yourself, do you?'

The tight feeling in his chest that had driven him from the living room reminded him once more of its presence. 'No.' He gave her a smile that he knew held no amusement whatsoever. 'I find myself very dull.'

'I don't.' The expression on her face was searching. 'I'm going to be your wife, Rafael.

Shouldn't a wife know a little more about her husband?'

He didn't want to talk about himself, not when there was nothing interesting about him or his past. Then again, he knew more about her than she knew about him and that didn't seem fair. And she was right; she would be his wife, so perhaps he could give her a little more?

'Fine,' he said. 'What do you want to know?'

Her mouth curved. 'Anything.'

'All right.' He stroked his thumb absently over the silky skin of her wrist. 'I could start with my father, though what to say about him that you don't already know? He used to visit me when I was growing up in Barcelona. Never at the apartment I shared with my mother, only ever in his territory, which was the hotel where he met my mother. I wasn't a son to him. I was an object to gloat over, a reminder of his own prowess, and really, it was pity that I was a mistake. I would have made a much better king than his legitimate child.' He couldn't hide the bitter edge in his voice, so he didn't bother. 'My mother, on the other hand, was decent. She didn't like me, but she cared for me all the same. She fed and clothed me, taught me right from wrong. Saw me as well educated as she could manage.'

*She never loved you, though, and why would she?*

He knew why. But that wasn't his truth to tell.

'She died when I was eighteen,' he went on, conscious of a certain tension gripping his muscles, an ache he hadn't even been aware of until this moment. 'Is that what you wanted to know?'

# CHAPTER EIGHT

RAFAEL'S EXPRESSION WAS so neutral as he said the words, his tone so casual. As if none of the things he said had any real meaning. As if they didn't touch him in any way.

But she knew they did and the signs were there in the burning silver of his eyes. Anger, hot and deep.

It made sense though, that he was angry. Why wouldn't he be? Carlos was always going to be a terrible father and then losing his mother. A mother who hadn't liked him...

That felt personally painful to her, though she had no idea why.

He'd never mentioned a word of this in the nights they'd spent together, talking and arguing about everything under the sun except their personal lives.

'I'm so sorry,' she said thickly. 'I didn't know.'

'Why would you?' His expression betrayed nothing, his tone mild. 'I didn't tell you.'

She stared up into his face, searching. His childhood must have been painful and yet he sounded casual, the way he always did. 'That must have been awful.'

He lifted a shoulder. 'No more terrible than other people with bad parents. It was all so long ago anyway. It doesn't matter now.'

It did matter, though, she could sense it. And now that she looked past the careful, expressionless mask he always wore, she could see it in his eyes, too.

'If it doesn't matter now,' she said quietly, 'then why are you still angry?'

Rafael's gaze flickered and she knew she'd struck a nerve. 'I'm not angry.'

'Like you weren't upset just now?'

'Lia—'

'Why do you always do this?' she said before she could think better of it. 'Why do you always pretend that nothing's wrong? You start talking about painful things as if you're asking for milk in your tea.'

His expression hardened. 'If you don't like

the way I talk about certain topics, then perhaps you shouldn't ask questions about them.'

*Why are you pushing him now? It won't help anything and it'll only make him angry all over again. You'll have plenty of time to talk about this later.*

That was true. And it seemed a pity to shatter the fragile sense of closeness they'd shared with an argument.

She already knew that they could argue with each other well enough, but what she really should be finding out was what they'd be like when they weren't arguing.

Lia pulled her hand out of his grip and laid it on his chest, feeling his warmth and firm strength. 'I'm sorry. If you don't want to talk about it, then we won't.'

His expression remained impassive, no hint of what he was feeling escaping, yet his gaze was so fierce. How could people not see how brightly he burned? They thought he was so cold and hard, but he wasn't.

He was a volcano in an ice field and lava gleamed beneath the snow.

Then unexpectedly, he put his hand over

hers where it rested on his shirt, his palm warm. 'I shouldn't have snapped at you, *princesa*. The truth is…that is not an easy part of my life to think about. My mother did not want a child. My birth was not her choice. But she had me anyway and cared for me as well as she could. It was upsetting when she died.'

Shock rippled through her. Not so much for what he'd said, but for the fact that he'd said it at all. And prefaced it with an apology.

But this was a gift, wasn't it? He was giving her something of himself and this time she hadn't had to ask for it.

It left her with other questions, such as why a mother would make it obvious to her child—to her blameless little boy—that he hadn't been wanted.

Lia had never chosen for this pregnancy to happen, but she couldn't imagine not wanting her baby, let alone making it clear to them that they weren't a choice she wanted to make.

'I can imagine,' she said carefully, before pausing and thinking a moment. Then she went on a little hesitantly, because she wasn't sure if this was something he'd considered or not. 'Rafael, I…do want this baby. You know that, don't you?'

His thumb moved gently, stroking her hand where it lay beneath his. 'I assumed so, since you are still pregnant.'

'Well, it's true. My parents had difficulty conceiving and eventually they had to do it via IVF. And when I found out that I was pregnant, I…was upset. But I knew immediately that I would keep it, because it was yours.' Her throat closed, realisation settling down inside her even as she said the words. 'This baby is a gift, Rafael. It's a gift for both of us.'

The look in his eyes shifted, some deep, powerful emotion rippling at last across his blunt, compelling features. He said nothing, letting go of her hand, but only to reach for her, drawing her in close, that hot, bright gaze on hers.

He didn't know what to say, she understood that. Or, no, perhaps it was because there was *too* much to say and he didn't know where to begin, or even that he didn't have the words for it.

But she knew one thing at least: what she'd said had meant something profound to him.

'It's all right,' she said softly, so that he didn't have to. 'You don't have to say anything. Just know I believe that with all my heart.'

His clothing was cool and damp where it pressed against her, the effects of his being out in the snow, but already she could feel the incredible heat of his body burning away the cold, burning into her.

Her only covering was the throw she'd wrapped around herself and she was still cold from her brief exposure to the outside air, but now he was warming her up. Making her feel hot and breathless and ready for him once again.

'This marriage of ours will work, Lia.' His voice was rough and demanding and full of an iron determination. 'I'll make sure of it. For the sake of our child's happiness.'

'Yes,' she said simply, because how could she argue against their child being happy?

She couldn't and she didn't want to, even if some small part of her ached for reasons she couldn't articulate.

Rafael's expression changed, his brows drawing down. 'You're not convinced?'

Damn. How had he managed to pick up on that sliver of doubt? Especially when she hadn't said anything aloud?

'Of course I'm convinced.' She tried to sound firm. 'Did I say I wasn't?'

'No, but your expression would say otherwise.'

Lia cursed herself silently. She'd become very good at hiding her emotions, at locking them down, so good that even those closest to her hadn't known when she was in a temper or upset.

Well, everyone except Rafael. She didn't know how he did it, but he always knew.

She stared at her hands where they were pressed to the crisp cotton of his shirt, trying to figure out why she was reluctant to tell him. Because what did it matter if she did? Weren't husbands and wives supposed to be honest with each other?

'Oh,' she said on a long breath. 'I was simply hoping that there might be some happiness left over for us, too.'

His hold shifted on her, one long finger catching her beneath the chin and tilting her face up so his hot gaze met hers. 'Did you think I would leave you out of the equation? No, *princesa*. I know what it is to have a desperately unhappy mother and I wouldn't wish that on any child, still less our own. So all you need to do is tell me what you want and I'll give it to you.'

*You want his heart.*

The thought came out of nowhere and she shut it down hard. Because, no, she didn't want his heart. Her feelings for him were large and powerful, but it didn't involve hearts, not at all.

'What I want is for you to kiss me,' she said, instead, and it wasn't a lie. She did want that.

So, he bent, his mouth brushing over hers in a surprisingly delicate kiss. Her lips tingled from the slight pressure, the heat of him warming her straight through and making her hungry for him again.

She shouldn't have these doubts. They'd have all the time in the world to discuss them later and, anyway, it would be all right. This marriage between them *would* work. What with her stubborn determination and his cold focus, how could it not?

'You won't regret it,' Rafael said as he lifted his head, a fierce expression rippling over his face, as if the door to a furnace had been opened and the heat of the flames had licked out. 'I promise, Lia, that I will do all I can to make you happy.'

He meant it, she could see the resolve in his face, and it made her chest go tight. What more could she want?

*You want love.*

Lia ignored the thought, since it was wrong. She already had love from her parents and that was enough of a burden to bear, heavy as it was with expectations and pressures. She didn't need that same burden from Rafael.

Instead she rose on her tiptoes and lifted her chin, brushing her mouth over his. 'You'd better start now, then,' she murmured. 'Because I'm deeply regretting the fact that you're not kissing me.'

'Then I'd better remedy that, hadn't I?' he said, before sweeping her up in his arms and carrying her upstairs to his bed.

Rafael was feeling well satisfied about a great many things by the time they came back downstairs to the living area.

Lia had picked up his discarded shirt from the bedroom floor and had put it on as if it was hers, a possessive gesture that made him want to take her back to bed and teach her a few more new ways to pleasure each other. Except they were both ravenous and she, especially, needed something to eat.

He led her back out into the living area where the refreshments had been laid, making her sit on the couch while he brought her more food. Then he sat next to her and asked her questions as she ate, because he wanted to know how her pregnancy had been.

He'd promised her she'd never regret agreeing to be his wife and he wanted to start by making sure she was well physically.

Luckily, apart from some early morning sickness that had faded, things had gone fairly smoothly, though it was clear as she talked, that she'd found her situation distressing in the extreme.

He could understand that and he understood, too, why she'd thought marriage to Matias was the only answer. She'd wanted to protect her baby and that was the best way to do it.

Still, he was here and now he would take care of both of them.

He sat back on the couch and watched her as she sat cross-legged, the sleeves of his shirt rolled up, taking delicate bites of the sandwich she was in the process of eating.

She looked very young and very beautiful, reminding him once again of the young woman behind the desk in her father's study, challenging him with a lift of her pointed chin and a glint in her blue eyes. Making him have to defend his arguments and explain his thinking. Forcing him to think past his own natural arrogance and his tendency to reduce things to black and white.

He hadn't thought one young woman could have taught him so much about himself and the flaws in his thinking, yet she had.

*'I know the treasury needs money,' Lia said, waving her cigar at him. 'But how do you balance that with what the people need?'*

*'Do the people not need money?' He took a sip of his own whisky, irritated that he had to explain himself. 'Santa Castelia's treasury has been decimated by Carlos's rule. That's why I was brought in, Lia. To help fill the coffers so when Matias takes over, he can implement all the social programs he wants.'*

*Lia shifted in the armchair, leaning forward to put her elbows on the desk, her blue eyes glowing with fervour. A strand of black hair fell over her face, but she made no move to push it back. She held his gaze without fear, as if he wasn't the ruler of her country and not given to taking kindly to people disagreeing with him.*

'But people need some of that money now. Leaving it in the treasury won't help anyone.'

'Interest will be accruing—'

'The poor can't live off interest accruing.' She met his gaze head on. 'You need to implement some of those social programs now.'

Rafael stared back, for a moment unable to think of a single thing to say because no one had ever interrupted him before, still less about fiscal policy. Oh, people did challenge him on occasion, but it was always very carefully done and often in the form of 'advice' rather than a command.

But not Lia. Out in the palace she might be shy and quiet, saying nothing, but in the privacy of Gian's study, she wasn't like that at all. She was blunt with her opinions and passionate, with a strong sense of justice and fairness.

She was...magnificent. And he found that he liked hearing her opinions. He liked arguing with her. He liked being challenged by her, even if it irritated him. It kept him on his toes, kept him sharp, and he hadn't realised how much he'd needed that until now.

'Social programs require money,' he pointed out. 'Which the treasury doesn't have.'

She waved that away as if it was nothing. 'But can't we do both? Can't we implement some for the most needy while keeping an eye on the bottom line?' Her cheeks had gone pink, passion glittering in her blue eyes. 'Why does everything have to be one or the other? The world isn't black and white, Rafael, so why do we have to do things as if it was?'

He was riveted, despite himself. 'So how would you suggest we go about it? Given how depleted the treasury is and how many loans the country has at the moment.'

Her gaze narrowed and she stared at him for a long moment, obviously thinking hard. Then she took a sip of her whisky, put the tumbler down. 'I don't know,' she said honestly. 'But if you give me a couple of days to think about how to do it, I'll bring you a plan.'

He couldn't refuse. He didn't want to. 'Do it,' he said. 'And if it looks like it could work, I'll implement it.'

* * *

The next night she'd come to him with a plan and—with a few tweaks—he'd been as good as his word and had implemented it. And it had been a success.

She'd encouraged him to think about more than just numbers and figures. About the people his policies affected.

*She is wasted on you...*

No, he could use her. Put that clever mind of hers to work for him. Be his right-hand woman in the boardroom as well as the bedroom.

She finished the sandwich and put her plate down, giving him a look from beneath her lashes. 'You're looking very pleased with yourself. What have you just been thinking about?'

'You and what an asset you are.' He leaned over to the table to pour some more orange juice into a glass for her. 'You probably haven't had time to think about what you might like to do with your future, but I wonder if you'd consider a role in my company.'

Surprise rippled over her lovely face. 'You mean work for you?'

'Yes. Why not? I can guarantee it would be challenging and exciting. You'd enjoy it, I think.'

She blinked. 'Oh… And what about our child?'

'There are many options we can consider. A nanny or we can have the child at work with us.' He handed her the orange juice. 'I am the boss, after all, and I can arrange it to suit our needs whatever they are.'

She took the glass, sipping carefully, watching him over the rim, her expression thoughtful. 'And where would you consider us living?'

He shrugged. 'Anywhere you like. It would probably be polite not to live here after Matias becomes King. I'm not sure he'd like the former Regent looking over his shoulder.'

'Did you ever want to be King?' she asked. 'Or consider changing things so you could take the throne?'

He didn't even have to think about it. He wanted nothing of his father's, especially not his crown. 'No. Matias will be a good king when he gains a little confidence and I'm ready for other challenges.'

Lia tilted her head. 'Why did you agree to be Regent?'

It was a good question and one he saw no reason not to answer. 'Because someone needed to fill Santa Castelia's treasury and someone needed to guide Matias.'

'Yes, but why you?'

He raised a brow. 'You think I wasn't a suitable choice?'

'No, it's just… Well, it's clear you have no love for Carlos, so why bother with his crown?'

This was edging into uncomfortable territory, but again, there was no reason not to tell her. She'd been so honest with him after all and, besides, it was no secret.

'I wanted to set an example,' he said. 'To show Matias what a ruler should be. Steady and calm, and absolutely in control of both himself and the country.'

'Ah, yes, that's what you're doing with this marriage, too, aren't you?'

'Yes. People need to see that I am nothing

like Carlos. And they need to see it in Matias as well.'

She gave him a slightly puzzled look. 'But it's obvious you're nothing like him, Rafael. Everyone can already see that.'

*Can they, though? When even your own mother couldn't?*

The unease inside him wound deeper, making the anger that had always burned sullenly in his heart flicker into life. He'd felt it out in his office, too, when he'd told her about his parents, about his father's egregious behaviour with him and his mother's dutiful care.

That Lia could see it had made him uncomfortable and he'd been glad when she hadn't pushed for more. So glad he'd given her another little tidbit just to show his appreciation. She'd been so sweet, too, putting her hand on his chest, pressing herself against him, her eyes full of sympathy.

He'd liked that. It had made the cold, icy part of him feel warm, which was perhaps a bad thing since his emotions had to remain frozen. Then again, channelling them into physical passion with a woman who wanted him, with his soon-to-be wife, wasn't wrong. And as long as he could keep doing that, everything would be fine.

*What if she wants more?*

Rafael pushed that thought aside, because really, what more could she want?

'That's because I work hard to make sure that's all they see,' he said casually. 'My father's genes aren't exactly easy to overcome.'

Lia blinked. 'Your father's genes?'

'He was a man very much driven by his not-inconsiderable hungers, *princesa*. Surely you remember? He was entitled, arrogant, selfish and had no self-control whatsoever.'

Her forehead creased. 'I don't remember much. I was young when he was King.'

Of course, she'd been a child.

*So very unsuitable for the likes of you.*

Rafael shifted on the couch, ignoring the thought. 'You didn't miss anything.'

She gave him an oddly searching look. 'Self-control is important to you, isn't it?'

'Naturally. It's the only thing that stops us from becoming animals like Carlos.' No, there was too much bitterness in his voice.

He needed to change the subject. 'You must think it's important yourself,' he went on. 'Or did your father know that the Crown Princess regularly drank whisky and smoked cigars in his office after hours?'

Colour flickered through her face, her gaze dropping abruptly to her hands where they held her glass of juice. She did that a lot, he noticed, especially when she wanted to hide something from him.

'No,' she said. 'He didn't. I didn't tell him.'

There was a faint edge in her voice which was interesting.

*You only think you know her, but you don't.*

He shifted on the couch again. He'd thought that before, that he was guilty of treating her like everyone else, ignoring her like everyone else. She was so self-effacing, so uncomplaining, so biddable and good, yet she was none of those things and he knew it.

And suddenly he wanted to know why. Why she'd sneaked into her father's study. Why she drank whisky, smoked cigars, and argued with a man years older than she was. Why she pretended she was the queenly equivalent of wallpaper, when she was as far from wallpaper as it was possible to get.

He'd always thought she'd be an excellent queen, but now, abruptly, he'd changed his mind. She couldn't be a queen. It would kill her.

Queens had to be controlled and well behaved, and in Santa Castelia's case they had to give way to the King.

Lia was wasted in that role. She should have been the King, not the Queen.

'You're very worried what your parents think of you, aren't you?' he said. 'Why? You're your own woman, Lia.'

'Why?' She looked up and stared at him very directly. 'Because they tried so hard to have me. Years of tears and heartache. And then they finally conceived me and they had a plan for me, and they loved me. How could I not do what they wanted? After all they went through to have me?'

'Yes, I can see that. But don't forget, it was their choice to have you. And you're not their property. You are your own person, with your own thoughts and feelings. You don't owe them anything.'

She swallowed. 'But… I love them.'

Love. Love was always the problem, wasn't it?

'You can love them and still have a life of your own.'

'I know… I just… I just wish that that was enough for them. That I was enough for them.'

There was a raw feeling in his chest. 'You're enough for me,' he said before he could stop himself. 'You always have been.'

She said nothing, staring at him, her expression unchanging, her blue eyes full of something he didn't understand, but it was fierce.

Then a tear slid slowly down her cheek.

Rafael felt as though someone had stabbed him.

*'Mi princesa,'* he said softly, hoarsely. 'Lia, did I hurt you?' He reached for her, unable to stand that look on her face, and drew her into his lap.

She was so small and delicate, yet she burned so hot.

His chest felt tight, his throat dry. He touched her cheek, felt the wetness of her tears. An ache spread out inside him, deep and intense. The same ache that had filled him when his mother had told him the truth about his father and what he'd done to her.

He didn't like it. He didn't want it, yet it filled him. Pain for another person, because they were hurt.

*Because you care.*

The cold he'd felt out on the terrace was back, winding through him, a chill that went bone deep. He didn't want to care. Caring hurt, caring made you vulnerable. If he had any kind of sense, he wouldn't be holding her like this. He'd be keeping his distance, changing the subject, making himself hard and cold.

Yet he couldn't let her go. She was in pain. She hurt and he wanted to know why.

'What is it?' he murmured. 'Did I say something I shouldn't?'

Mutely she shook her head. Then, before he

could say anything else, she flung her arms around his neck and pressed her face to his throat.

For a minute he sat there, stunned. No one had ever put their arms around him like that. Not as if they wanted his comfort. As if he had something to give that was more than money or power, or an example to set.

His heart beat furiously, the ache pervading every part of him.

He wasn't sure what to do next, not when this was so outside of his experience.

Except, no, that was wrong. An instinct that he didn't even know he possessed told him that he knew exactly what to do. So, he obeyed it, wrapping his arms around her and gathering her close, holding her.

For long minutes they sat there like that, the softness of her gathered against his chest, close to his heart. And his chest was so tight he couldn't breathe, some immense emotion pressing against it. An emotion so strong, so vast, he couldn't fight it.

He let it pulse through him, hot and intense, because in this moment it didn't matter what he felt. She was the most important thing in his universe and he would never, *ever* hurt her.

Then she turned her wet cheek and her mouth burned against his skin.

And the flames took hold.

She was so sweet, so unbearably sweet.

He felt as if he was melting, frozen pieces of himself warming up and thawing, the feeling inside him escaping, permeating every part of him.

He slid his fingers into her hair and held on tight, devouring her mouth as one by one the checks he had on his control began to fall. And he let them go. He couldn't stop this need, couldn't fight it.

She was on her back on the couch, his shirt ripped from her body before he knew what was happening. And for a second, he found himself in the depths of winter again, frozen with a sudden terror that he'd done something she hadn't wanted, that he'd been so overcome with need he'd missed some cues.

But then she reached for him, her blue eyes glowing with heat, clearly unbothered by his intensity, the way she'd always been unbothered by it.

'I need to be careful with you,' he heard himself say in a voice that didn't sound like his. 'Lia, you must tell me if I'm too much.'

'You're never too much,' she murmured. 'Never.' Then she pulled him down.

And there was no stopping after that, no holding back either.

He'd somehow got rid of his clothes and then he was pushing inside her, feeling the slick heat of her hold him tight, melting the last cold parts of him.

Her arms were around him, her thighs closed tightly around his hips, and she was moving with him, her gaze on his a bright gas-flame-blue. There was so much pleasure, his whole body filled with delight, with heat and with passion.

'I want you,' she whispered and the fire that had been part of him, that he'd always denied, finally escaped, blazing bright between them.

And he let himself be consumed.

# CHAPTER NINE

LIA LAY IN the huge bath and looked out the window at the snow outside. It had stopped falling, but the drifts were still huge, lying thick and deep against the sides of the trees, the house and the corners of the window.

There was something particularly delicious about lying in a warm bath while looking at an icy landscape and Lia took full advantage of it.

Rafael had suggested a bath before dinner and even though she'd already had a shower earlier, the thought of lying in some warm water was pleasant enough that she'd let Constanza run one for her.

Rafael himself had wanted to check any communications from the palace and the various media outlets to get an update on their situation with the outside world, so he'd disappeared into his office.

She rested her head against the black marble of the tub, staring at the window, her head full of him.

Rafael, sitting on the couch with her as she ate, handing her more food and pouring her orange juice. Rafael, telling her that she was enough.

Rafael, putting his arms around her.

Rafael, telling her that she was enough for him, as if there was nothing attached to it, nothing she needed to do to earn it. As if it just was.

She hadn't meant to cry when he'd said that, but it had felt so painful and at the same time so unbearably sweet that she hadn't been able to stop herself. A strange and intense feeling had swept through her that she couldn't have articulated even if she'd wanted to.

And it was still there, lying heavy in her chest, that familiar nagging ache that had now become part of her.

It had been there for a long time, maybe even that first day she saw him getting out of the limo, but back then she hadn't recognised it. It had felt too big, too complex, too terrifying. She hadn't been ready, not when she was supposed to be marrying someone else.

Her eyes prickled and a tear slid down her cheek, joining the warm bathwater.

How ridiculous to cry about falling in love, because that's what this was, wasn't it? Not a teenage crush or mere physical desire.

It was love. She loved him. There was nothing else this deep, intense feeling inside her could be. And he'd showed her what it meant.

It meant being accepted for who she was, without expectation, without pressure. Without having sad stories of sacrifices made and heartbreak overcome just so she could exist.

Her hand slid over the gentle swell of her stomach.

It was the way she would love her child, too.

She sat there for long minutes, her tears falling slowly, but they weren't tears of sadness or despair. They were more for the intensity of the bittersweet joy inside her. Joy, because he made her happy. Bittersweet because she had no idea how he felt about her.

He wanted her, of course, and she thought

he cared about her wellbeing, but did he feel this same ache that she did? And if he did, did he know what it meant? Probably not, considering his past.

Not that it mattered.

None of her previous concerns mattered. Being Queen, having a future, the press, being chosen. They were all petty problems that paled in comparison to what she felt for him.

She closed her eyes, remembering how he'd taken her on the couch with a fury and intensity that her whole soul had gloried in.

It amazed her how he could think he was in any way like his father and believe it, yet it was clear that he did believe it.

She wanted to know why. Had someone told him he was like Carlos? Was that the issue? And if so, who?

It made her furious, made her want to shout at whoever was responsible, because he wasn't like his father, not in any way. His self-control spoke of a very deep and intense desire to protect other people, which was a foreign concept to Carlos.

Perhaps what Rafael needed was simply someone to tell him, to show him what a good man he was. Strong and principled, and perhaps on the outside a little hard, but with a caring heart underneath that.

Well, she would be that someone.

Matias had needed a queen, but Rafael needed *her.* And while he might not ever say 'I love you' back, he needed her all the same and she knew the truth of that with every part of her.

Eventually the water cooled and she hauled herself out, drying herself off and going into the bedroom. He'd turned the heating up further, so she didn't need the sweatpants and hoodie combo, but she had to put on something.

She was in his bedroom, a huge room with vast windows that looked out over the mountains. A massive bed was pushed up against the wall facing the windows, the frame heavy oak. A matching dresser, just as massive, stood against another wall, a door beyond it that must lead to an en-suite bathroom.

The decor was dark and luxurious, charcoal-greys and dark blues, and very masculine, and Lia liked it very much. Especially when she could smell the faint hint of his delicious aftershave in the air.

The shirt of his she'd been wearing before was presumably still on the floor of the living area downstairs, so she went over to the tall dresser of polished oak that stood near the bed.

After a brief investigation of the drawers, she found a soft T-shirt that looked comfortable, so she pulled it out. Then something caught her eye.

A photo frame had been tucked beneath a layer of neatly folded shirts.

Lia frowned and pushed aside the fabric.

It was a photo of a beautiful woman with black hair and the same grey eyes as the little boy she was crouched next to, her arms around him. Both the woman and the boy were smiling at the camera, the swings and slides of a children's playground behind them.

A little shock went through her as recognition dawned.

This was a picture of Rafael and his mother,

wasn't it? The mother who'd never wanted a child and who'd never liked him, or so he'd said. The mother who was nevertheless holding him and smiling.

'What are you doing, Lia?'

Lia froze as Rafael's deep voice came from the doorway, her heart kicking in her chest. She felt oddly as if she'd been discovered doing something she shouldn't, which was ridiculous when she'd only been looking for something to wear.

She turned around to face him.

He'd taken a few steps into the room, his expression merely curious rather than angry.

'I was trying to find a T-shirt to wear,' she said. 'Sorry, I didn't mean to intrude on your privacy.'

He lifted one muscular shoulder. 'This will be your room, too. No apology is necessary. Did you find one?' His gaze fell to the still-open drawer and the photo in it, no longer buried by clothing. He went abruptly still.

Lia felt the temperature of the air plunging as if he'd opened the door to the outside and all the snow was blowing in.

She took a small breath. This photo meant something to him obviously, but nothing good, that was also clear.

*He is hiding something from you.*

Oh, she knew that already. And she'd pushed her instincts to ask him about it to one side, telling herself that there would be plenty of time later to discuss it. And she still could. She didn't have to push him now and what would it accomplish anyway?

*But isn't this what you've been doing all your life? Doing what other people want. Doing what you're told. Doing what's expected of you. How does that help? What does it achieve?*

A shiver of realisation went through her.

Nothing. It achieved nothing and it changed nothing. It didn't make anything worse, but it didn't make it better either.

*Is that what you want your marriage to be like? You avoiding tackling painful subjects because you don't want to rock the boat? What are you afraid of?*

Oh, but she knew the answer to that. It had been inside her this whole time if she'd only been brave enough to look. Except she'd never been brave enough until now. Until she'd fallen in love with Rafael Navarro.

Her fear was there, a cold kernel in her heart, of not being the good, quiet girl her parents wanted her to be, of not meeting their expectations. Of disappointing them after they'd endured so much to have her.

The fear of not being good enough to love on her own.

So she'd tried to mould herself into what they wanted, being good and quiet and bidable. Making them proud.

Except she wasn't like that with Rafael, she never had been, and anyway, she didn't know how he felt about her, so what did she have to lose?

She loved him and her fear didn't matter in the face of that. The only thing that mattered was him and if she wanted to help him, take away his pain, she was going to have to push.

Determination settled down inside her.

'Is that a picture of you and your mother?' she asked.

His gaze had gone a dark, gunmetal grey,

the door to the furnace of his intensity firmly closed. 'Yes. Did you find a T-shirt?'

It was very clear he was not going to talk about the photo.

'I did,' she said. 'It's a lovely photo, Rafael. Why is it at the bottom of your drawer?'

He pushed the drawer back in. 'Because that's where I put it.' He turned toward the doorway. 'Constanza will be serving dinner shortly. Shall we go down?'

It was clear that it was not a request.

Lia didn't move. 'The moment you saw it, I could feel the temperature of the room plunge about fifty degrees. Why is that?'

Again, he lifted a negligent shoulder. 'I'll tell you about it later.'

'No. You will tell me about it now.'

He was halfway to the door and he stopped. His back was rigid, every line of him stiff. 'I'm not sure I like you demanding answers from me.' That casual tone was back and she hadn't realised before how much she hated it.

'You're doing it again, making it sound like you don't care,' she said flatly. 'Except I know that you do. What is it with your mother, Rafael?'

He turned his head to the side, the muscles in his jaw tight. 'You'd prefer it if I shouted at you? Perhaps throw things like a child?'

But she could see past that reserve, could see beneath the ice field. She'd always seen the fire in him, no matter how deep he buried it beneath layers of ice.

'Being angry doesn't make you Carlos,' she said quietly. '*Nothing* you do will ever turn you into him.'

Something clicked into place inside her all of a sudden. His apparent coldness in stark contrast to the passion that burned inside him. The way he always sounded casual when there was something vital to be discussed. The quiet, frightening way he'd issue orders or warnings. He never lost his temper, not once. He was always in control.

*Except with you.*

*'I think you're wrong,' Lia said flatly, staring straight into Rafael's silver eyes. She hadn't known where she'd got her courage from,*

*whether from the whisky bottle in front of her or from the rush of adrenaline that had filled her the moment she'd uttered the words.*

*It was a challenge and they both knew it.*

*'I'm wrong?' he echoed in that mild tone he always used and yet that always sounded so menacing. 'Are you sure?'*

*He was sitting sprawled in the chair opposite, the buttons of his shirt undone, his sleeves rolled up, relaxed and so unbelievably attractive she could hardly breathe.*

*'Of course you're wrong.' She had to say it again, just to see the silver in his eyes flare and because she liked saying it. Like poking the tiger sitting across from her with a stick. 'Money isn't the be all and end all.'*

*He tilted his head. 'Says the woman who's never been hungry a day in her life.'*

*She flushed, because of course that was true. 'I'm not saying money isn't useful and that it doesn't buy a certain amount of happiness. But that happiness isn't lasting.'*

*'But doesn't that depend on how much money you have?'*

*'Fine.' She put her elbows on the desk and*

leaned forward, bracing herself and looking into those fascinating eyes of his, feeling her heart begin to hammer in her head at the risk she was taking. 'Then, given how much money you have, are you happy, Your Excellency?'

'Of course,' he said in that same tone.

If she hadn't been gazing straight at him, she wouldn't have noticed the flicker in his gaze, but she did notice.

'Really?' She didn't move. 'What makes you happy, then?'

'This is an irrelevant conversation.'

'No, it's not. Unless you're not telling me the truth.'

He looked away, stubbing out his cigar in the ashtray, then taking a last sip of his whisky. 'You'd better start talking about something interesting, princesa, otherwise I have other things to be doing.'

'You're not happy,' she said, watching his face and making a guess, amazed at her own audacity for questioning him. She shouldn't step outside the box of demure princess and *she knew it, but she couldn't stop. 'And you don't want to talk about it.'*

*He pushed his chair back, rising to his feet. 'I think that's enough for one night.'*

*She didn't move, the need to keep pushing him, dig beneath the surface of him and find the fire that burned in his heart too intense. It was there, she knew it, she only had to keep digging. 'What are you afraid of?' She threw the question at him like a stone and then, because she somehow always went too far, she added, 'Rafael.'*

*He'd already turned to the door, ready to leave, but the sound of his name made him stop. And for a second she thought he'd stride out without a word.*

*But he didn't.*

*He turned back to her, so fast she barely had time to take a breath before he was right in front of her, leaning his hands on the desk, bare inches away, those silver eyes so close she could see the striations of charcoal running through them.*

*'No, princesa,' he said, his voice not so casual now, but edged with a slight roughness.*

'These kinds of topics are off limits, do you understand?'

Her heart was beating so loudly she could hardly hear him. He was so close. All she needed to do was to lean forward slightly and her mouth would brush his. 'What topics?' she asked hoarsely, unable to look away.

'Anything to do with our private lives.'

'But what if I want to? What if I—?'

'Then I will not come to see you any more.'

He meant it, she could hear the flat note in his voice, the hint of steel.

'You don't mind me...arguing with you, though? Or disagreeing with you?'

Again, that flicker in his gaze and this time it was accompanied by a slight relaxing of that hard, implacable mouth. 'That, I do not mind. In fact...' He paused and for a second the whole world faded away, just simply ceased to exist. There was nothing else in it, but the burning intensity of his eyes. A molten, burning silver. 'I like it.'

A second later, he'd pushed himself away and was gone, leaving her sitting alone in the study, staring at the door he'd disappeared *through, her heart fluttering around like a butterfly trapped in a net.*

*Everything felt darker and colder when he wasn't here. Everything dull and muted.*

*She was right, though, wasn't she? There was fire in him and it burned so bright. And now she'd seen it, she was going to make it her mission to make it blaze every single time....*

And she had. He was never reserved and cold with her after that night and she couldn't let him be anyway. She'd flung challenge after challenge at him, letting him blaze and blazing along with him.

But he'd never shouted when he got passionate about an argument. He'd get up and pace and sometimes those silver eyes of his would get molten, but he was nothing like Carlos.

'I know I am not my father.' Again in that dangerously mild tone.

'Then why do you pretend that nothing touches you?'

'You think I'm pretending?'

She almost laughed. 'You think you're not?'

'Lia, I don't see—'

'What happened with your mother, Rafael?' She cut him off, suddenly knowing that if she didn't crack that icy exterior of his now she never would. That he'd be closed off to her for ever and she couldn't bear that, not for his sake and not for hers. 'And don't lie to me about how it doesn't matter. If it really didn't matter, you would have just answered the question.'

It was dark outside, the light in the bedroom dim. Yet he could see Lia's face and the determination written all over it with absolute crystal clarity.

She always looked that way when she was determined to challenge and push him, and most of the time he'd let her. Except there were some things he didn't want to discuss with her and that photo was one of those things.

It was a picture of one of the happiest times in his life. When for whatever reason, he was never sure, his mother had taken him to the playground. And for an hour or two it was as though she'd forgotten what he represented, as if he was simply her son and she loved him, not the constant reminder of the worst moment of her life.

He'd kept that photo because it was the only one he had of her smiling and it had felt important that he remember that smile, especially when he could count on one hand the number of times she'd smiled at him.

But he didn't want to tell Lia that.

He didn't want to discuss his mother with her at all.

'Fine,' he said casually, because all he had about this particular topic was casual. 'You're right, that's me and my mother. I keep the picture to remind me that she was happy once.'

Lia's expression turned suddenly soft, that almost tender look crossing her delicate face. The one that made his chest feel as if an iron band was crushing it. 'She looks very happy. She must have loved you a lot.'

'I think you're assuming she felt some motherly feelings towards me.' He bared his teeth in a facsimile of a smile. 'She did not.'

The soft expression on her face faded. 'What do you mean she did not?'

'I told you earlier. She looked after me because it was her duty, but there was too much of my father in me for her to care about me.'

Lia's blue gaze widened. 'She actually said that to you?'

'*Si.* And often.' So he'd tried to prove to her that he was nothing like Carlos. Endlessly. Trying hard not to lose his temper, trying hard to do what he was told and study hard, and treat his mother gently and kindly. To make up for the sin of being born.

Then she'd died and he didn't have to do it any more, but by that stage he'd realised that the easier way was just to cut those feelings out of his heart. To not feel them at all.

So, he hadn't.

'Oh, Rafael,' Lia murmured, crossing the distance between them. 'That's awful.' She put her hands on his chest, her palms warming his skin through his shirt. 'Why would she say that?'

He wanted to be angry, to hold on to the sullen, burning flame in his heart, but he couldn't. It felt as if the pressure of Lia's hands were stripping that anger away, leaving underneath the raw wound of the truth.

A truth he couldn't tell her, because it was his mother's and she was gone.

All he had left was the half-truth.

'Because she was angry that she had me. She had…plans for her future and I got in the way.' He brushed a strand of black hair back behind her ear, unable to stop the casual touch. 'She didn't like me making a fuss or throwing a tantrum or being difficult. She would tell me I had to be careful, that I had to be measured and considerate in my behaviour in case I turned into Carlos.'

The crease between her brows deepened. 'But…kids are like that. I was like that.'

'Not all kids. She set an example for me and I followed it.' He reached for her wrists, circling them with his fingers and pulling them gently away. 'Let's have dinner. It'll be on the table by now.'

But Lia's chin had a familiar stubborn slant to it. 'What kind of example? I mean, that's ridiculous. You don't have to practise not being like Carlos, Rafael. You just *aren't* him. Why on earth would you think that you are?'

The heat smouldering inside him flared. 'It wasn't my mother's fault. I was an angry child and that only got worse as I got older. I was wilful, stubborn and I had a temper, just like Carlos had a temper, and that frightened her.'

Lia was still frowning. 'But all children throw tantrums. And being wilful and stubborn aren't exactly unusual traits.'

The hot coals that sat in his gut glowed hotter, the iron band around his chest tightening yet again. Anger and pain, two things he'd cut out of his heart and never wanted to feel again.

Clearly it was time to end this conversation.

'Do you have a point, Lia?' He tried to keep his tone moderate the way he always did. 'Our dinner will get cold and Constanza will not be impressed.'

'I don't care about Constanza,' Lia said. 'I'm still trying to figure out why you think you're like your father.'

'What does it matter?' Impatience was

creeping into his voice. 'Carlos is dead and so is my mother.'

'Yes, but you're not. So why are you acting as though they're still alive?'

His patience began to thin. 'I don't understand what you're talking about. I know they're not alive. Do you think I'm stupid?'

She paid no attention to his tone. 'No, of course not. But you do know what I'm talking about, Rafael. You're so cold, so detached. And that's not who you are.'

'I'm not detached. I'm simply in control of my emotions.'

'In control,' she echoed. 'Was that what kidnapping me from the cathedral was all about? You being in control of yourself?'

He could feel all his muscles tighten yet again, the tension excruciating. 'We have been over this. You're pregnant with my child and I had to do something—'

'You stopped a royal wedding. In the middle of the ceremony. And then you—'

'What is your point?' He'd taken a step toward her before he knew what he was doing. Adrenaline coursed inside him, making him feel hot, making him feel the need to do something intensely physical just to get rid of it. 'You want a fight, *princesa?* Is that what you're trying to do?'

Lia took a step toward him, in no way cowed by him. Her eyes were glowing with that intense blue light that always filled them when they were challenging each other.

*You're fiery and hot, the pair of you.*

No, maybe she was, but he wasn't. He was the master of himself. He had to be.

'What I'm trying to do,' she said fiercely, 'is to get to know my husband. You told me months ago that you didn't want to discuss anything private or personal and I agreed. But things have changed.' She took another step. 'We're going to be married, Rafael, and you are going to be a father. I think the time for that embargo on private conversation is over.'

He could feel his temper fray, responding to the glint in her eyes and wanting to answer it. But he couldn't.

*His mother, crouching down in the ruins of his bedroom, looking at him with fear in her eyes. Her grip on his shoulders was so hard it was painful. 'Rafael, do you really want to be like your father? Violent and horrible? Hurting people the way he hurt me? Is that who you're trying to be?'*

*His rage had burned out, leaving him hollow and empty, and he couldn't remember any longer what he'd even been angry about. Now all he felt was fear.*

*'No, Mama,' he said, his throat sore from shouting. 'I would never hurt you. I want to be a good boy.'*

*Her mouth was a hard line, her eyes full of a terrible ferocity he didn't understand. 'Then you have to control yourself. You* must. *You cannot get angry like this any more. Because one of these days you will hurt someone. You* will *hurt me.'*

*'I'm sorry, Mama,' he said, because at seven years old, all he wanted was not to hurt his mother. 'I'll try hard not to, I promise.'*

*She stared at him. 'You can't escape who you are, Rafael. You were born with your father's flaws, so you will have to do this all your life. Understand?'*

Oh, he'd understood. At first control was his lord and master, but over the years, he'd mastered it. He would not let that temper get the better of him, especially not now, with this woman in his keeping.

A woman he'd promised to himself never to hurt.

'Please, Lia. Do not push me.' He put everything he had into keeping his tone level, to not letting the pressure of the heat inside, the hard, violent emotion he knew he couldn't let off the leash, not ever. 'We need to have this conversation at a later time. First, there is dinner—'

'Stop talking about dinner!' She was close to him now, all soft and warm in his T-shirt. She smelled like the bath oil she'd used, something sweet that set all his senses alight, no matter that he'd spent hours sating himself on her body already. 'I don't want this conversation at a later time. I want it now. Because if you can't have it now, you never will. And I'll never break through all the ice you're surrounding yourself with.'

His patience thinned to snapping point.

'You think you can order me around? Tell me to talk to you and I will? Like a good little lapdog? Is that what you think?' He closed the remaining distance between them, inches away from her, burning up from the inside. 'Who gave you the right to demand anything you want from me?' He could hear the anger in his voice, the heat bleeding through. 'Why do you think you deserve to know?'

She didn't look away from him, her own special brand of ferocity burning in her eyes. 'Because I'm going to be your wife, Rafael.' Her cheeks were pink, the blue of her gaze as deep and dark as a midnight sky. 'And... because I love you.'

It felt as though she'd slipped a knife between his ribs.

*You can't have love. You don't deserve it.*

'You don't love me,' he snapped, not acknowledging it because if he did perhaps it would go away. 'You just love the pleasure I give you.'

She went white. 'What do you mean by that?'

'You're a good girl, sheltered. Cosseted.

You've never known sexual pleasure until I gave it to you.' The words spilled out of his mouth, harsh and sharp and cutting. 'It's very common for virgins to confuse love with passion and I'm sorry, but that's what happened to you.'

The fierce look in her eyes didn't change, she only looked at him and he could hear his own words coming back to him, tinny and cruel and wrong.

Then her hand came out unexpectedly and touched his cheek and he felt that knife twist beneath his ribs, pain radiating out. 'You want to believe that, don't you? You want to believe that very badly. Why?'

He reached for her hand, pulling it away from his face. 'This isn't about me.'

'Of course it's about you. I know what I feel, Rafael. I know my own heart and I've loved you for years. Before I even knew what love was. It's you that doesn't know, I think.' Gently she pulled her hand out of his hold and touched him again, just a brush of those cool fingers. 'Tell me, has anyone said that to you before? Has anyone told you that they loved you?'

His stomach dropped away, every part of him in agony. 'Why would they?' he heard himself say. 'Why would anyone?'

A terrible sympathy crossed her face. 'No one? Not even your mother?'

'Let me tell you what I was to my mother,' he said, the words coming out before he could stop himself, even though it was a truth that wasn't his to give. 'I was the living reminder of what my father did to her. Of how he hurt her.'

Lia frowned. 'What do you mean?'

'She was a hotel chambermaid,' he said, because now he'd started down this path he had no other option but to keep going. 'My father regularly stayed at the hotel where she worked and he decided he wanted her. She was very strong willed, however, and she wouldn't sleep with him, so he courted her. He couldn't marry her, because he was a king, but my mother disapproved of sex outside of marriage and so refused him. She loved him and he told her that he loved her, but still she refused.'

He bared his teeth. 'So, he got her drunk one night and raped her. Afterwards he held her and told her she was beautiful and that he loved her and that it would all be okay. He manipulated her into thinking nothing had happened. She thought it was all fine because she loved him and he loved her, but when she told him that she'd conceived, he gave her some money to make her go away. And that's when she realised she'd been used.'

Lia went pale, her expression horrified. 'Oh, Rafael…'

'So, no, no one ever told me that they loved me. Why would they? Why would anyone love a child that came from that?'

# CHAPTER TEN

LIA STARED IN shock at him, that deep, vast emotion pressing against her heart, making it ache, making it hurt. Making her want to put her arms around him and hold him, keep him close.

'Oh, Rafael… Oh… I'm so sorry…'

The look on his face was terrible. 'I was the living reminder of what had happened to her, of why her life was ruined. She knew how I was conceived, could see the flaws in me, the same flaws my father had, and she taught me that I had to be better. That I had to learn how to control them otherwise I'd turn into him. And I tried. I did my best never to get angry, never to hurt her. She looked after me dutifully but I could understand why she never loved me. Why would she?'

There were tears in Lia's eyes, his tall figure wavering. Her chest felt as though it was full of barbed wire, the sharp points digging into her heart, pressing hard enough to draw blood.

No wonder he'd had no reaction to her telling him she loved him. And no wonder he'd told her that it was just physical passion.

He didn't believe in it because he'd never experienced it.

After what had happened to his mother, love for him was nothing but hurt.

Her throat felt tight and sore, but she forced the words out. 'You were a child, Rafael. You were blameless and your mother had been hurt very badly. It wasn't your fault.'

His mouth twisted. 'I ruined her life, Lia. Every day she looked at me, she could see my father. She could see what he did to her. And when she saw the same traits in me that he had, it terrified her. *I* terrified her.' His eyes had gone dark. 'I promised I would make our marriage work. I promised that I wouldn't give you a moment's regret, that I would make you happy, but… I've never made anyone happy. I don't know how.'

Her throat closed. She knew where he was

going with this, she could sense it. 'You do,' she said forcefully. 'You *do* make me happy. You told me I was enough for you, that I was an asset. You accepted me as I was when even my own parents didn't.'

'It's not enough though, is it?' His voice was harsh. 'You love me, Lia. But I do not have the first idea of how to love you in return.'

'I don't need you to—'

'Yes,' he cut her off roughly. 'Yes, you do and you want it, too. Why do you think you did everything your father asked? Why do you think you went to the altar to be married? You want to be loved, *mi princesa,* and you deserve it. You deserve it so much. But I am not the man to give it to you.' He paused. 'I can't marry you, Lia. I'm sorry.'

The pressure in her chest became crushing. 'I don't understand,' she said, even though she had a horrible feeling that she did. 'I thought… I thought you wanted to marry me. I thought that I was yours.'

Slowly, he shook his head. 'I am poison. I hurt people the way I hurt my mother. I swore never to hurt you, but I will. One day I will and I cannot have that. This is the only way.'

Her throat had gone tight, her heart scraped raw. 'So, what? This is all about protecting me?'

His hands had curled into fists at his sides. 'You are so young. You have a life ahead of you and years to find someone else. I am flawed. Too flawed.' His eyes had darkened ever further, all that blazing silver doused. 'If I take you now, how am I any better than my father? Giving in to his emotions, giving in to his own lusts. Taking without asking and not giving anything in return. And you need that, *princesa*. You will suffocate without it.'

There were more tears, she could feel them sliding down her cheeks, her heart tearing itself to pieces as the future she'd only just started to imagine for them both slowly shattered into a million diamond-bright shards.

She wanted to be angry, to rage at him, tell him he was a fool and wrong. That she didn't care if he didn't love her. That being with him was all she wanted and he didn't need to give her anything.

But it was clear he wasn't going to listen. He preferred the ice he'd buried himself under and who was she to argue? Who was she to push?

She had no right to him or his feelings, and the only thing she had to give him was her love. And that wasn't enough.

'But what about the baby?' Her hand rested on her stomach, grief tearing at her. 'Your son or daughter will need their father.'

The silver of his eyes had died completely, they were the colour of ash now. 'It would be better if my child never knew me. I am not an example they should be following. But don't worry, I won't leave you with nothing. You will be taken care of.'

'Rafael, no,' she said hoarsely. 'You can't.'

'I can.' A muscle leaped in his jaw. 'It is my final word.' He took a step back, away from her. 'You may stay here for as long as you wish. I'll deal with the outside world. You can leave that side of things to me.'

Lia nodded, barely hearing him. She felt cold all of a sudden, as if winter had come into the room, scattering snow and ice everywhere, the bitter chill making its way inside her and freezing the ragged pieces of her heart. She didn't know what to say. Not that she could have said anything anyway. It was clear his mind was made up and she couldn't change it.

He was the product of a terrible act, the way he saw himself set in stone right from a young age. And she couldn't blame his mother for that. She'd had a terrible experience and Lia could understand her grief and her fear. That she'd put it on her son was awful, but knowing that wouldn't change what had happened. Wouldn't change the past.

And it wouldn't help Rafael.

He wasn't poison. He was the antidote. He'd given her freedom within the cage she'd been trapped in and some of the purest moments of happiness she'd ever known.

She would do the same for him if only she knew how.

'You should eat,' he said at last. 'You'll be hungry.'

'No,' she said. 'I'm not. I think I need to go and lie down.'

Then she fled from the room before he could stop her.

It was late, midnight possibly, but Rafael didn't bother looking at the clock. He'd long since ceased to care. He sat in his office, staring at the bottle of good whisky on top of his desk, every part of him wanting to drink the entire thing, while his control told him no.

It felt important to resist. He *had* to. Because if he didn't, if he gave in, what was to stop him from going upstairs and dragging Lia from her bed and into his, and keeping her there all night?

Keeping her there for ever.

But he couldn't. Her tears had nearly killed him, the lost look in her eyes when he'd told her that he would never love her making him feel as if his heart was tearing itself apart in his chest. Yet it didn't matter how much pain he felt, he couldn't give in to that need.

He couldn't give in to the feeling inside him, the intensity, the ferocity. That feeling damaged people. That feeling hurt people. And it would hurt her if he wasn't careful.

'People do terrible things in the name of love,' his mother had said, when he was thirteen and in the grip of his first crush. 'You especially will have to be careful.' And then she'd told him the story of his conception. The reason why he was so very flawed, why she couldn't ever love him the way he always wished she could.

He'd been appalled. Shocked. Disgusted. And he'd sworn he'd never do what his father did. He would never give in to his own feelings, take what wasn't his.

And love especially he would avoid like the plague.

Nothing had changed since that day, no matter how Lia insisted. It hurt her, yes, but keeping her, knowing he could never give her the one thing she deserved above all else, would only hurt her more.

This was the right decision. The only decision.

His phone rang and he'd hit the answer button before he'd fully thought through the wisdom of it.

'So, Zeus told me what was happening,' Vincenzo said without any preamble. 'And I wanted to call you to tell you what a terrible idea—'

'I'm returning her to the palace,' Rafael snapped. 'As soon as the weather clears.'

Vincenzo was silent for a long moment, shock echoing down the phone line. 'You're returning her? But isn't she pregnant?'

'Yes. I can't marry her, though. And it was wrong of me to take her.'

Another long silence.

'I'm sorry, but I thought I heard you say that you were wrong.'

He gritted his teeth. 'I was.'

'Why?'

Rafael didn't want to have this discussion. Vincenzo had just married the woman he'd fallen in love with and probably wouldn't be here for his thoughts on the nature of love. 'Because she loves me.'

'Obviously a cardinal sin,' Vincenzo murmured dryly. 'And I suppose you're returning her now because she deserves better?'

Rafael glared at the desktop. 'She does.'

'Ah.' Vincenzo sounded as if he'd just discovered something very interesting. 'I see.'

'You see?' Rafael growled. 'What do you see?'

'You're in love with her.'

His heart froze, everything froze. 'No.'

'Yes, you fool. Of course you are.'

'What makes you—?'

'Because that's what I did with Eloise. You send them away, telling yourself you're protecting them, but it's not to protect them. You're protecting yourself, because you're in love and you're damn terrified.'

Rafael's heart felt like a block of ice in his chest. 'I can't,' he said roughly. 'Love makes people do terrible things. You know Carlos. You know what he was like. You know—'

'Oh, please,' Vincenzo said in some disgust. 'I wouldn't have thought you of all people would let that old bastard define who you are.'

'I'm not,' Rafael ground out.

'You are. Do you really think you're capable of hurting someone? That you would ever hurt her?'

'I'd rather kill myself than hurt her. That's why I had to send her away.'

'Dramatic, but that answers that question.' Vincenzo's voice was bone dry. 'You're afraid, Rafael. And you're using your father as an excuse. And that I understand. But it's not only you that you need to think about. Doesn't she deserve love?'

The block of ice around his heart began to soften, gradually, slowly.

Lia, sitting in that armchair with whisky and a cigar.

Lia, eyes glowing, arguing with him.

Lia, in his arms, passionate and loving.

Lia, looking at him. *I love you, Rafael.*

Who had ever loved him? Not his father. Not his mother.

Lia, looking at the photo of his mother with her arms around him. *'She must have loved you...'*

*If you were all bad, why is she smiling?*

*'You were blameless, a child. And she was damaged...'*

His heart shifted, shuddered.

'Yes,' he said hoarsely. 'She does.'

'Then stop putting yourself and your fears first and think about her.'

Was that what he was doing? Was that all this was? Just fear?

Fear that he was actually as bad as his father. Fear that he was poison. Fear that there was nothing but flaws inside him, that he wasn't worthy of anyone's love.

Except... Lia did love him. Lia had loved him for years.

She wasn't afraid of him. She never had been. Not of his anger or his passion or the ferocity inside him, the intensity. No, she'd simply matched it with her own. They were the same, weren't they?

Both passionate, both strong. And she wasn't poison, so... Why did he think he was?

*You do love her.*

He could feel it now, the fire of that love, heating him up, melting the ice. Warming his soul all the way through.

There was nothing toxic in it, nothing poisonous. It felt...clean.

He couldn't know that for sure, but...maybe if she wasn't afraid, then he didn't need to be either. Maybe, if he trusted in her strength and her bravery, he could trust himself, too.

'Rafael?' Vincenzo demanded. 'Are you still there?'

'I'll call you back,' Rafael growled down the phone. 'I have a wedding to organise.'

# CHAPTER ELEVEN

LIA WOKE TO brilliant sunshine. The world outside was blindingly white, snow everywhere, but the blizzard had vanished.

Snow was piled high on the mountains, weighing heavily on the trees, and probably covering all the roads, but it was clear enough that a helicopter could get through, because she could hear the rhythmic sound of the rotors through the trees.

The outside world intruding.

Rafael, leaving.

Her eyes filled with tears and she wanted to turn over and bury her face in her pillow, the ache in her chest filling the whole world.

She would go on—she had to, especially now she was a mother—but something inside her had broken irretrievably and she knew that nothing was going to fix it.

It was her heart. And it would never be whole again.

At that moment the door to the bedroom opened and Constanza came in, her arms full of something white.

Lia blinked. 'What is that?'

The housekeeper laid the white thing down on a nearby chair. It appeared to be a white gown trimmed with silky white fur. 'For you,' she said. 'You have fifteen minutes.'

'Fifteen minutes?' Lia echoed blankly. 'For what?'

'No time to explain.' The housekeeper beckoned. 'Come on, I'll help you with the buttons.'

Lia didn't want to. Yet it was clear Constanza wasn't going anywhere, so reluctantly she dragged herself out of bed.

'You can have a shower,' the housekeeper said. 'But make it quick.'

Five minutes later, cleaner but no less mystified, Lia found herself being buttoned into the white gown. It was made of thick white silk, with voluminous skirts, and fitted her small bump to perfection. It was long sleeved, with a deep V at the neckline.

After Constanza had buttoned her into it, she folded a white fur cloak around Lia's shoulders and gave her a pair of white boots to put her feet into.

'Is this...?' Lia began to say and then faltered.

Constanza merely turned towards the door. 'Follow me.'

And Lia did, half in a daze, not understanding what was happening, though a part of her knew. A part of her had recognised that this was a gown and it was wedding white.

But she didn't want to think about it, didn't want to hope, so she followed Constanza down the stairs and into the living area, where the doors to the terrace outside were already open.

Chilly wind whipped through the open door, the terrace outside sparkling in the winter sunlight.

Shining on the man who stood by the parapet waiting for her.

He was dressed in black and he was staring at her, his grey eyes molten silver. He was alone.

'Rafael...' Her voice failed, her throat going thick.

'I'm sorry, Lia,' he said, his voice that rough velvet she loved so much. 'I am so sorry about last night. I kept things from you, hid things from you. What happened to my mother was her story and I didn't feel I could tell anyone, but... I felt you needed the truth. And here is another truth.' His eyes blazed. 'I love you, *princesa*. I have loved you for a long time, I think, but I didn't recognise it for what it was. I was afraid. Afraid that if I opened myself up to it, I'd lose control, become something terrible like Carlos. But it was you who showed me differently. You who made me see that love isn't something to be afraid of, that it isn't pain and suffering. That it is healing and warmth and strength.'

Lia's eyes were so full of tears, she could barely see his tall figure in front of her. 'Why? What changed?'

'A phone call from an old friend.' His expression softened just a touch. 'Yes, I have friends.'

She swallowed and then she was walking towards him, her feet crunching in the freshly fallen snow. 'You're not like Carlos, Rafael. You know that, don't you? You finally believe it?'

'*Sí.*' The fierce heat in his eyes had something else in it now, not just pain, but something more. Something that wasn't desperation, but a certain kind of peace. 'And because I am not my father, if you do not wish to marry me, you can walk away. Say the word and you'll never have to hear from me again. I'll leave you to make your own choices, to follow your own heart.'

Lia blinked hard through her tears, meeting his gaze. 'I've followed my heart already. That's why I'm standing here.'

A fierce expression crossed his face, part-possessive, part-protective, all love. 'Are you sure? You don't have to choose me if you don't want to.'

Even now, he was holding himself back. Foolish, stubborn man.

Her throat was tight and sore, but there had never been any doubt about the feeling in her heart. That this man was worth the fight to have him.

And there would be more fights in the future, because no relationship was ever a simple bed of roses, but she knew in the deepest heart of her that she would battle to keep him with her last living breath, because he was worth it no matter the cost.

'I do want to,' she said simply. 'And I choose you, Rafael. I will always choose you.'

He lifted a hand, not taking his gaze from hers, and from out of the house came three men. All tall. All ridiculously handsome—one was even wearing a crown.

The dark-eyed man in the crown came to stand next to Rafael, while the other man, dark-haired and wearing sunglasses, came to stand on the other side.

The third man, again dark-haired and dark-eyed, with olive skin, who wore his immaculate suit with a certain careless insouciance, gave her a smile that if she hadn't been about to marry the man she loved would have knocked her socks off. 'Your bride, Rafael,' the man said, 'is exquisite.'

'Stop trying to charm her, Zeus, and marry us,' Rafael growled.

Lia coughed delicately. 'Rafael…'

'*Mi princesa,*' Rafael said, sliding an arm around her waist and drawing her close. 'These are my friends, Vincenzo and Jag.' He indicated the man wearing the crown and the man in sunglasses. 'And my other disreputable friend Prince Zeus, who has been ordained and can marry us.'

'This is much better than the cathedral,' Lia said and leaned against her husband to be. 'Yes, please marry us, Prince Zeus.'

It was a very quick ceremony and afterwards there was champagne. Lia thought Rafael might want to spend time with his friends, but they didn't linger. Vincenzo had his own wife to get home to and Zeus and Jag had other 'adventures' to attend, according to Zeus.

Lia had her own adventure, too.

There were many things to organise, many

issues that needed to be handled, but Rafael ignored all of them in favour of sweeping her up his arms and carrying her to his bedroom.

And they began their future together right then and there.

# EPILOGUE

RAFAEL WOKE WITH a start to find the bed empty. He thought he might know where Lia was, so he got out of bed and went downstairs, and sure enough, his wife was sitting on the couch, their son and daughter in her arms.

The twins had obviously just finished a feed and, miracle of miracles, were lying there quietly.

He leaned in the doorway a moment, taking in the sight of his brand-new family. Twins had been unexpected, but he and Lia had coped and their birth had indeed been the gift she'd promised it would be.

As was she.

The fallout from his kidnapping her had been intense and people had talked of nothing else for a good month. It had helped that Matias had given his blessing almost immediately, telling Rafael that, actually, it had felt like a weight had lifted off his shoulders and that he had someone else he'd had his eye on for quite some time.

The transition of power had been smooth. Matias had become King and he'd promptly married the woman he'd loved since he was a boy, whom no one knew about.

Lia's parents had been disappointed, but not for long. Not once the twins had been born.

All in all, it had worked out very well.

Rafael moved into the room and went over to the couch. Lia looked up and smiled, the love shining in her eyes making him ache.

But it was a welcome pain, a sweet pain.

And when he took his daughter in one arm and curled his wife and son in the other, he let it flow through him.

He'd started out with winter in his soul and Lia had been the spring, thawing him out.

Now it was summer and he knew there would be sunshine to the end of his days.

Sunshine in his heart for ever.

\* \* \* \* \*